The Orloj of London

The Orloj series: Vol. 4

Erasmus Cromwell-Smith II

The Orloj of London

ISBN: 979-8-9989106-4-7
Publisher: Erasmus Press
Proofreading: D. Suster, Tracy-Ann Wynter, Janet Bartos
Cover Design and Interior Design: Elisa Arraiz Lucca
www.erasmuscromwellsmith.com
First edition
Printed in USA, 2025.

Books written by the author

In English,   **En Español,**

As Erasmus Cromwell-Smith II:

The Equilibrist series,
(Inspirational/Philosophical)
-The Happiness Triangle (Volume 1).
-Geniality (Volume 2).
-The Magic in Life (Volume 3).
-Poetry in Equilibrium (Volume 4).

(Young Adults)
-The Orloj of Prague (Volume 1).
-The Orloj of Venice (Volume 2).
-The Orloj of Paris (Volume 3).
-The Orloj of London (Volume 4).
-Poetry in Balance (Volume 5).

As Erasmus Cromwell-Smith

The South Beach Conversational Method
(Educational)
- Spanish
- German
- French
- Italian
- Portuguese

The Nicolas Tosh Series, (Sci-fi)
- Algorithm-323 (Volume 1).
- Tosh (Volume 2).

As Nelson Hamel (*)

The Paradise Island Series, (Action/Thriller)
- Miami Beach, Paradise Island (Volume 1).
- Dangerous Liaisons: Miami Beach (Volume 2).
- The Rebel Hackers of Point Breeze (Volume 1), (Sci/fi).

(*) in collaboration with Charles Sibley.

All titles are or will be available in audiobooks

Como Erasmus Cromwell-Smith II:

La serie El Equilibrista,
(Inspiracional/Filosófico)
-El triángulo de la felicidad (Volumen 1).
-Genialidad (Volumen 2).
-La magia de la vida (Volumen 3).
-Poesía en equilibrio (Volumen 4).

(Jóvenes Adultos)
-El Orloj de Praga (Volumen 1).
-El Orloj de Venecia (Volumen 2).
-El Orloj de Paris (Volumen 3).
-El Orloj de Londres (Volumen 4).
-Poesía en Balance (Volumen 5).

Como Erasmus Cromwell-Smith

El Método Conversacional South Beach
(Educacional)
- Inglés,
- Alemán
- Francés
- Italiano
- Portugués

Table of Contents

Note by the Author,

No city on Earth is more paradoxical for an Orloj quest than London—where no single famous astrological clock stands, yet illusions thrive in every corner. If you've traveled with these six young wizards through **Prague's medieval illusions, Venice's watery labyrinths, and Paris's hidden clock towers**, you already know that each city's magic demanded deeper moral truths: from humility to loyalty, from compassion to respect. Each triumph awakened a stronger bond between these friends and tested them further against an adversary hungry for any failing. Their efforts paid off: in **Prague**, they earned **Wizard Apprentice** status; in **Venice**, they rose to **Young Wizards**; and in **Paris**, they attained the rank of **Master Wizards**.

Yet none of the prior Orloj adventures fully prepared them—or me—for London's complexity. This metropolis hides its "astrological clock" behind legends of Big Ben and centuries of secret illusions: a place where the swirl of time warps around Tower ravens, and echoes of monarchy and monarchy's betrayals can break even the proudest wizard. Here, illusions lurk beneath unassuming facades; old mentors appear with cryptic riddles, or vanish into swirling gusts before we realize they were ever truly there. Dark forces—like **the relentless Goblin**, who survived Prague's tunnels, Venice's labyrinth, and Paris's illusions—sense that this city is our culminating test.

Each virtue we earned must now shine stronger than ever, or be devoured by illusions that know our every doubt.

Across these pages, the Harlequins—older and warier—face a twenty-four-hour countdown that surpasses every trial they endured in Europe's famous clock cities. **London lacks a single, grand Orloj façade**, yet its intangible "clockwork" churns relentlessly, ready to measure each flaw or virtue we dare to show. Summon everything gleaned from the prior three books: generosity vs. greed, honesty vs. betrayal, humility vs. arrogance, respect vs. apathy, and more. In London, the illusions burrow deeper, demanding not just the mastery of spells but a mastery of self.

May you enter this hidden capital, feeling the hum of gears that no tourist sees and the silent chimes that echo at the brink of dawn. If **Prague taught us to discover our moral foundations, Venice proved unity's strength, and Paris refined our perspective on compassion and respect**—then London will reveal what happens when all those virtues meet a city of illusions with no single clock **face**, but countless reflections of our own hearts. Time's final test is here. Let us begin.

—Erasmus Cromwell-Smith II.

PREFACE

Isle of Skye, Scotland (Summer 2058)

The rugged cliffs of the Isle of Skye plunged dramatically into the restless waves of the North Atlantic, shrouded in a mist as ancient as the rocks themselves. Here, silence spoke louder than words, broken only by an occasional seabird's cry or the wind's gentle murmur through the heather-covered hills. The place felt primal, as though it were quietly observing those who walked its edge.

Professor Erasmus Cromwell-Smith II and his beloved companion, **Lynn Tabernaki**, trod a narrow trail that clung to the cliff's edge, absorbing the serenity of the Scottish highlands. The prior summer had been all whitewater adrenaline; now they sought a more contemplative journey—exploring ancient ruins, tracing paths among standing stones rumored to pulse with a faint magical resonance.

That evening, nestled in their secluded cottage overlooking the sea, **Erasmus** lit a modest fire. **Lynn** watched him from a cushioned chair, recognizing that familiar introspective hush that overcame him each year as a new academic cycle neared.

"Ready for another nostalgic dive into your wizarding past?" she teased gently, sipping warm tea.

Erasmus managed a soft smile, eyes reflecting the flames. "Indeed," he replied quietly. As the embers crackled, old memories stirred.

Lynn tilted her head. "You never shared much about **London** last year," she pressed, carefully measured. "What made it so different?"

Erasmus let the question hang for a moment, gaze drifting. "London was… *singular*. We weren't Young Wizards any longer—this city tested us in ways no one anticipated."

Intrigue piqued, Lynn ventured, "Another series of hidden clocks and Orlojs, I suppose?"

Erasmus chuckled softly, eyes glinting with distant recollections. "Yes, only… London's clock was hidden more deeply. No single great 'astrological clock' stands in that city. Yet illusions thrived in every corner, and old mentors arrived more mysteriously than ever. It was a journey of illusions and truth, betrayal and loyalty, virtue and vice."

Lynn leaned forward, curiosity shining. "So, you reached another level of wizardry?"

A cryptic smile crossed Erasmus's features. "**Beyond Master Wizards**. The city demanded a deeper magic—a profound responsibility that changed us forever."

As **night settled** over the cottage, Erasmus rose, moving to the window. Moonlight bathed the cliffs in pale silver, the sea whispering far below.

"And like Prague, Venice, and Paris," he said, voice subdued, "I've told no one about the full scope of London's trials. The memories waited here"—he tapped his chest— "until now."

Lynn's smile widened. "Then I'll be present again, as always. Even if only *virtually*."

Erasmus squeezed her hand. "I would expect nothing less."

The moonlit hush over Skye gave way to the waning days of summer. Morning after morning, Erasmus and Lynn strolled the heathered ridges, her gentle questions drawing forth scattered fragments of his London memories. Each evening, the wind off the Atlantic seemed to carry whispers of the Orloj's hidden chimes, spurring him to make notes for his upcoming lectures. By the time the leaves hinted at early autumn, Erasmus felt equal parts nostalgia and anticipation—the perfect balance to begin another academic year.

A few days later, the cozy stone cottage was but a warm memory as he boarded the Hyperloop from San Francisco to the Central Institute of Arts and Literature. Checking his watch, he was amused—and only mildly irritated—to see he was seven minutes behind schedule. Some things never changed.

Central Institute of Arts and Literature (Fall 2058)

The Hyperloop from San Francisco hummed through its vacuum tube, whisking **Professor Erasmus Cromwell-Smith II** to his annual academic pilgrimage. Dressed today in deep burgundy tweed, he felt the usual tingle of excitement as the institute came into view.

"On my way," he texted Lynn, the corner of his mouth lifting.

Her reply was immediate: "*Surprise, surprise, you're running late.*"

Rolling his eyes playfully, he stepped from the Hyperloop moments later, *exactly seven minutes tardy*. Some traditions never changed. Students and VR participants thronged the auditorium, **five hundred** in person and countless more connected remotely.

"Welcome back!" he greeted, projecting warmth that reverberated through the hall.

"Great to be back, Professor!" came the chorus.

Once they quieted, **Erasmus** regarded them with a spark in his eye. "This year, we journey once more into my past—into a chapter I've kept cloistered; let me take you back to the summer of 2033. *At fifteen,* my companions and I found ourselves in **London**, a city lacking a singular grand astrological clock, yet teeming with illusions that dwarfed everything we'd experienced. *Here,* we reached beyond mere Mastery."

He paused, scanning the sea of eager faces, each leaning forward in anticipation.

"Poetry and timeless fables remain our guiding lights. Prepare for illusions that deceive, virtues that empower, and hidden truths. We shall peel back London's layers to discover the Orloj that mortal eyes never see."

With a subtle smile, he dropped his tone to an intimate

whisper. "**Join me** once more, as we uncover the secrets of London's Orloj. The story begins now…"

Prologue

Summer, 2033

A hush of **anticipation** lay over the Thames in the half-light before dawn. A faint, clinging mist hovered at the river's edges, waiting—just as London itself waited—for an extraordinary shift. Though the city's bustle continued, small pockets felt oddly suspended, as though *time itself quivered.* Under lampposts near the Tower of London, silhouettes flickered and dissolved; at a deserted corner of Paddington Station, a swirl of color sparked, then vanished. Subtle illusions whispered that something profound was about to unfold.

High on a terrace overlooking **St. Paul's** dome, **Mr. M.** stepped out of memory. A half-cape rustled around his spectral form—one of the old Equilibrist mentors, returning in ghostly cameo. With a half-smile, he raised a gloved hand, adjusting an invisible top hat, then turned skyward.

"They will be here soon… Balance, dear ones. Balance for the final act."

An instant later, he dissolved into ribbons of swirling color, leaving only the faint hum of distant traffic.

One year had passed since the six young wizards—**Blunt, Reddish, Firee, Checkered, Breezie, and Greenie**—achieved

Master Wizard status beneath the illusions of Paris's Orloj. Each prior city—Prague, Venice, Paris—had begun with a test, introduced virtues and flaws, then rewarded them with unity and new powers. Yes, they didn't vanish from each other's lives for a year. Though they'd all returned home after Paris, they kept their chat group alive. So, when the Orloj's subtle signs pointed to London, they arranged to meet once again. Now, as the next anniversary approached, their mentors hinted that **London** awaited: a seat of monarchy and mystery, where *no singular "astrological clock"* was known to stand.

Yet each Harlequin still felt the pull. Across the globe— Boston to Beirut, Barcelona to Shanghai—they sensed ephemeral signs. In fleeting dreams, a **Dark Goblin** skulked around a looming tower; cryptic text exchanges buzzed with both excitement and dread. "No big clock in London," Reddish had typed, *"so how does the Orloj appear?"* Firee pored over archives fruitlessly —**Big Ben** was famous, but not considered an *astrological* clock, nor rumored to hide magical gates.

Still, the Orloj's vow echoed in each of their minds:

"Where mortal eyes see none, the Orloj's presence can be found. Remain eager, remain bold… The next city awaits your spark."

Exactly at midnight, **Mrs. V.** emerged on an empty train platform in Brussels, a swirl of tattered fabric in her wake. Older and more translucent than any living person, her kind

gaze still shone bright. She watched a Eurostar rattle past—
Blunt dozing with a duffel bag in his lap—then whispered into
his dream:

"London awaits, child. Heed the smallest act of kindness or
faintest despair. Be vigilant—there is more to learn than ever
before."

She vanished, leaving Blunt to stir with a half-remembered
vision.

Meanwhile, at **Waterloo Station** in London, travelers bustled
off the late train from Dover. Near a defunct newsstand, bright
lights flared momentarily—a cameo of **Mr. N.**, wearing an old
RAF jacket. He gave a crisp salute, murmuring:

"Attend to your discipline, young wizards. London can
devour hope if you let it. Be on your guard."

Then he, too, blinked out of sight, leaving behind only a scrap
of a newspaper fluttering to the floor.

Throughout London, **subtle illusions** wove themselves into
the city's quiet corners, heralding the Harlequins' approach.
Beneath a flickering streetlamp, a twisted figure lurked—a
hooded Goblin with malevolent eyes. Surviving defeats in
Prague's tunnels, lurking in Venice's labyrinth, tasting defeat
in Paris, the **Dark Goblin** now paced near the Tower of
London, scraping his claws against cold stone.

"They come…" he hissed. "And I shall feast on their failings."

A flash of lightning split the clouds, and the Goblin retreated under a medieval arch, cackling softly. He felt sure that the Orloj's young Master Wizards would falter amid London's illusions.

Dreams of a Foretold Story

Morning broke in a bright hush over the skyline. One by one, the six friends arrived—some by foot, others by train or family car—converging near a worn statue by **Charing Cross**. Exhilarated greetings and tight hugs followed. Though each had grown slightly taller or changed in subtle ways, their bond felt as strong as ever.

Securing a pocket of privacy in a station alcove, **Blunt** drew out the same **blue-and-gold magical book** they had carried since Prague. Its pages fluttered with a hum of deeper power. Lines formed on a blank sheet:

"We meet again. Be ready: This city is different. Where no astrological clock stands, an Orloj forms anew. Six flaws, six virtues—ascend beyond Master Wizards… or face your downfall."

Greenie inhaled sharply. "Is this… truly the final step?"

Checkered frowned. "Maybe it's bigger than final. *Beyond Master Wizards?*

We're venturing into the unknown."

Reddish brushed hair from her face, voice certain. "No second-guessing. We face it together."

They exchanged determined looks. Around them, the swirl of morning commuters carried on. A lone busker strummed a soft tune. High overhead, **Buggie** (the Orloj's hour-hand son) buzzed gently, shining a tiny green laser at the direction of the Thames, while **Thumbpee** (the minute-hand son) popped onto Blunt's shoulder, folding his miniature arms with a brusque nod that said: *Time to go.*

Below, in a dim corridor, a tall man in a navy scarf watched. His form flickered half-spectral: **Mr. Ringwald**. His lips moved in silent caution: "Beware illusions of arrogance, dear wizards. Pride slays caution. London can host your triumph… or your ruin."

Then the station's lights dimmed for a split second; he was gone.

Thus, on that **summer morning**, the Harlequins stepped onto London's bustling pavements, hearts aflutter with anticipation and nerves. No imposing "astronomical clock" greeted them, but the city felt alive with possibility. A faint shimmer across the Thames suggested illusions, mentors, and old adversaries awaiting. They sensed that **the Orloj of London** promised a final test—one that would push them to surpass every limit they knew.

And somewhere in the city's hidden corners—amid Big Ben's chimes or the haunted stones of the Tower—magic stirred once more.

Let the final journey begin

Their journey converged as trains and cars bore them from distant lands to Waterloo Station, the city's pulse quickening with their arrival under a still-summer sky. And yet, something was amidst, their parents were not present to wave them off, neither their Chaperones!

Dreams…, Only Dreams (Not for long, though)

And then, as if pulled back from mist and magic, each of the Harlequins awoke. Blunt blinked at the ceiling of his London flat, heart pounding with the echo of Mrs. V's whisper still lingering in his mind. Reddish sat upright in her hotel room, breath caught in her throat as if the Goblin's glare had truly reached her. One by one, across the city's outskirts, they emerged from restless sleep—each having dreamt of train stations, mentors, and swirling illusions. They'd all experienced the same dream. A prelude of what was to come. They would meet soon, yes—but their mentors' messages had arrived in dreams, not waking reality. Each one of them with their parents in tow headed to King's Cross Station their agreed meeting point. The true reunion, they sensed, was just beginning.

Chapter 1

Arrival & Ominous Encounters

London's Hidden Orloj

Howling winds swept through London's streets, lifting scattered autumn leaves into spirals that danced wildly beneath dawn's nascent light. A lingering aroma of impending rain saturated the air, mingling with distant rumbles of thunder that grew steadily into roars. Dust swirled violently, obscuring the waking city in ghostly veils. Storm clouds gathered swiftly, the electrifying flashes of lightning heralding nature's fury.

Unlike Prague, Venice, or Paris—each boasting a famous astrological clock—London had no such renowned Orloj on display. *Big Ben marked the hours, yes, but rumor whispered that the city's true, hidden clock lay concealed behind everyday facades.* This peculiar void made London's magical presence elusive. Still, the dark forces lurking here felt anything but uncertain. They awaited eagerly, knowing the gritty young wizards were close. This confrontation would be unlike any before—the occult realm was restless and implacable, unwilling to suffer defeat again.

In hidden corners and forgotten alleyways, unique figures stirred: a Chimney Sweep paused briefly, glancing skyward with wary eyes; a Busker strummed softly, his music tinged with knowing melancholy; and a Raven Keeper whispered quietly to his birds, whose dark feathers bristled at the unseen energies. Even the venerable Tower itself seemed to shudder in anticipation. High above the rooftops, hopping from ledge to ledge with lithe grace, the mysterious Pied Piper played a haunting tune, its melody carried away by the strengthening winds. The city held its breath, poised on the precipice of extraordinary events.

The London Reunion

The steam hissed softly as the train glided into King's Cross Station, its wheels whispering against iron rails. Amid the bustling crowd disembarking onto the platform, six familiar figures emerged—each scanning the station with a mix of excitement and cautious apprehension. They were expected, and somewhere unseen, magic watched them closely.

Erasmus Cromwell-Smith II, aka Blunt, was the first to step forward, the Boston native adjusting his glasses while his sharp eyes meticulously swept the surroundings. Blunt was tall for his age, his demeanor always thoughtful, his dark hair habitually tousled.

Next to him stood **Sofia Martínez, aka Reddish**, the fiery-haired girl from Barcelona. Her green eyes glittered curiously, forever fearless, her freckled face lit with determination.

Close behind, **Sanjiv Patel, aka Firee**, the ever-alert wizard from Mumbai, moved gracefully through the crowd, his penetrating gaze taking in every detail, his features calm but guarded.

Winnie Mahlangu, aka Checkered, from Pretoria, followed confidently. The athletic girl's dark braids swung rhythmically with each decisive stride; a spark of humor ever-present in her deep, thoughtful eyes.

Quiet yet deeply perceptive, **Sang-Chang Liu, aka Breezie**, the wizard from Shanghai, appeared almost to glide rather than walk. His slender build and graceful demeanor belied the intense magical strength beneath his quiet exterior.

Lastly, **Carole Haddad, aka Greenie**, from Beirut, stepped gracefully onto the platform. Her expressive brown eyes, framed by rich dark curls, hinted at the intuitive sensitivity that defined her every move.

Hidden in shadows near the platform, the Dark Goblin hissed quietly, bitterness evident. "You think your unity makes you strong? It was unity that betrayed me. Friendship abandoned me, left me to darkness. You'll soon understand betrayal as I do."

Just as the youngsters exchanged excited greetings, **their parents emerged from all directions on the bustling platform**, relief and trepidation evident on each face. **Hugs came quickly**; whispered well-wishes mingled with anxious smiles. Even though everyone had witnessed hints of the Harlequins' magical calling in past adventures, the parents still felt a pang each time they let their children out of sight. A few **mothers blinked away tears**, while **fathers clapped shoulders with forced grins**. Yet the farewells, though heartfelt, were swift—these families **respected the Harlequins' bond** and trusted them to protect one another.

At the far end of the platform waited **Bart Sutton-Leigh**—Blunt's American uncle—and **Antonella Cromwell-Smith**—his Italian aunt—each stepping forward with a rare mix of **pride and deep concern**. They had watched these six grow from curious novices into capable young wizards, but the ache of letting them go never eased.

"We know how strong you are," Antonella murmured, voice taut with feeling. "Just remember—take care of each other."

"And come back in one piece," Bart added with a shaky laugh, giving Blunt a quick hug. "We'll be waiting in London."

With final nods of determination, the six friends shouldered their luggage and turned toward the next step of their journey—**carrying the warmth of these emotional goodbyes in their hearts**.

As the group split and everyone went their separate ways, Blunt sensed a subtle shift in the crowd. His instincts sharpened. In the blink of an eye, a familiar figure brushed past him—a fleeting shadow disguised as a busy porter.

"Beware, Blunt," the figure whispered urgently. Blunt's heart raced as he recognized the voice—**Mr. M.**, the Equilibrist mentor from his father's stories. "It all ends at the Tower. Yet, it does begin at Waterloo station."

Blunt froze, the station's clamor fading. His uncle's hug lingered—a warm ghost against the cold unknown. His heart thudded, eyes tracing the crowd. "We're not kids anymore," he murmured, voice rough. Reddish met his gaze, her nod solemn, a silent vow amid the bustle. The weight settled: this wasn't a game.

Before Blunt could react, the figure dissolved into swirling color, leaving behind only a hint of magic and a lingering chill. He exchanged silent, knowing looks with his companions. **They'd all mastered wizardry once before**, forging a unity that had guided them in their last trials, but London's Orloj promised an even deeper test—one that might push them beyond the boundaries of Master Wizards.

"Let's stay alert," Blunt cautioned quietly, his voice steady but charged. "Our adventure has begun," he cautioned everyone as he realized that the indicated alternate train station was located within walking distance.

A soft rumble of thunder rolled overhead, as though echoing his words. None of them knew *exactly* what the next level of wizardry entailed, but in a city with no obvious astronomical clock, they sensed that answers—and perils—awaited within London's hidden heartbeat.

Chapter 2

The Quest for London's Astrological Clock

Morning at Waterloo Station

After a 2.5 miles stroll, the group of 8 was about to complete the switch of train station.

Morning sunlight spilled softly onto the bustling platforms of Waterloo Station, where Blunt, Reddish, Firee, Checkered, Breezie, and Greenie stood alongside **Bart Sutton-Leigh** and **Antonella Cromwell-Smith**. Today marked the beginning of their quest to uncover London's *hidden Orloj*, guided only by subtle clues scattered among ancient astrological clocks—an approach that felt far more roundabout than their previous journeys.

Suddenly, **Breezie** stiffened, eyes widening as an ethereal figure materialized at the edge of the platform. It was **Mrs. V.**, her delicate swirl of fabric impossibly old yet luminous, defying the busy rush around her. Her gentle, familiar voice whispered clearly despite the noise:

"Seek first the court where tides and time entwine, where Henry's stars in copper shine."

Before Breezie could speak, the apparition vanished into a faint shimmer.

As Mrs. V. disappeared into the shimmering mist, Breezie's mind raced, repeating her cryptic hint quietly, *"Seek first the court where tides and time entwine, Henry's stars in copper shine…"*

"Did anyone else hear that?" Reddish asked, eyes scanning the bustling crowd.

"Yes," Blunt replied, his own eyes sharp with curiosity. "But what does it mean?"

"Tides and time…" Firee mused aloud, pacing thoughtfully.

"Copper stars," Greenie pondered, brow furrowed. "That must refer to something metallic, something historic."

"Henry VIII!" Checkered suddenly interjected. "It must be the astronomical clock at **Hampton Court Palace**—it's famous for showing tides on the Thames!"

The group shared relieved smiles, grateful for the mentor's subtle yet illuminating clue.

As they turned to head for their train, a *flash of malice* pricked Blunt's senses. Cloaked in the shadows beneath the station clock, the **Dark Goblin** glared, eyes glittering with contempt.

"Run while you can, foolish wizards," he hissed softly. "Your path leads only to despair."

A chill slithered through Blunt as he quickened his pace, almost able to feel the Goblin's gaze burning into his back.

Reddish froze mid-step, eyes darting toward a trench-coated figure looming near the station exit. "He's been following us," she murmured.

Greenie sensed a spike of malice emanating from him—an all-too-familiar swirl of illusory energy.

"Could be the Dark Goblin's decoy," **Blunt** whispered, clenching his fists. "Let's confirm."
With a quick nod of agreement, **Firee** and **Breezie** led the group in activating **invisibility**—one of their earliest powers from Venice. Their harlequin suits shimmered, turning translucent. **Checkered** urged caution: "Remember, if we stay hidden too long, the side effects…" A faint tingle pricked at their fingertips, but they advanced silently, weaving through unsuspecting travelers.

At close range, the trench-coated figure dissolved into a ragged swirl of illusions, cackling in triumph. **Only a decoy!** Anger flared in **Reddish's** face. "We nearly wasted time chasing a phantom." Yet the Goblin's ploy had been thwarted: the Harlequins emerged from their invisibility, hearts pounding. Exchanging tense nods, they hurried onward to catch the train for **Hampton Court**, determined not to let illusions slow them again.

Hampton Court Palace

The train rattled gently toward Hampton Court. Breezie gazed out the window, forming the shape of an hourglass on the condensation. "Do you ever wonder if we're ready for all this?" he murmured almost to himself.

Reddish, seated beside him, considered. "Every journey has made us stronger—but readiness? I think we're never truly ready. We just...become ready along the way."

Checkered nodded. "Like sands in an hourglass, always shifting, always moving forward—even if we're not ready."

Antonella smiled warmly, sharing an approving glance with Bart. "Exactly. Hampton Court Palace it is."

Blunt glanced at his friends, determination in his eyes. "Remember, everyone—unlike Prague or Venice, London doesn't have a famous astrological clock out in the open. Ours must be hidden, maybe even *virtual*, waiting behind a magical portal. If we find it, that could unlock the way into parallel London—and take us beyond Master Wizards."

They exchanged eager, confident smiles, understanding the stakes.

"Then let's hurry," Reddish urged, leading the way toward the waiting vintage steam train.

At Hampton Court Station, the group disembarked onto a quaint platform fringed by ivy-covered walls. Ahead rose the **Tudor grandeur** of Hampton Court Palace, its warm brickwork glowing in the midday sun. Upon close inspection nothing was what it appeared to be from afar. **A swirl of flames danced across the stone footbridge** leading to the palace grounds, crackling with menacing illusions. Behind it, tendrils of frost glinted like jagged shards. Passersby stumbled back in terror.

Checkered raised a brow. "This must be the Goblin's handiwork, blocking our route."

Reddish gave a half-smile. "He forgets we learned to walk through fire and ice back in Prague."

Without hesitation, they stepped forward. The illusions hissed, blazing tongues of fire licking at their ankles, while frigid air swirled around their shoulders. But the Harlequins pressed on—**their old power** made such elements harmless. Onlookers gaped as the group emerged unscathed on the far side of the bridge. **Breezie** shrugged off a final ember. "No more delays," he said firmly.

And so, they continued, unshaken, toward **Hampton Court**.

Once they reached the courtyard normalcy returned. Tourists drifted about, but the buzz died to a hush as the Harlequins approached the **renowned astronomical clock**, its gilded copper face adorned with zodiac signs, celestial symbols, and moon phases.

"There it is," Greenie breathed, eyes wide with awe.

"Why isn't it moving?" Checkered asked, puzzled.

Blunt rested his fingertips on the cool copper surface. A subtle tremor passed beneath their feet, and the air crackled with magic. *It knows we're here;* he thought.

A metallic creak pierced the silence, and the clock's dials spun wildly, signs dissolving into a blur. Then, just as abruptly, it froze—displaying **strange symbols** that looked indecipherable.

"I believe you might require assistance,"said a calm voice behind them. Turning, they recognized **Mr. Faith**—the antiquarian mentor from Boston, known for teaching *Clarity* and *Focus* on their last adventures.

Mr. Faith approached, eyes twinkling. "Observe closely," he instructed. "There's a *bishop's mitre, the moon at its zenith, and a pair of knights.*"

They puzzled aloud, until Checkered connected the symbols to **Wells Cathedral**, with its own knights on the clock.

"Precisely," Mr. Faith said approvingly. "Wells Cathedral awaits. Remember: clarity of thought—see beyond the obvious."

Mr. Faith's eyes darkened, voice low. "Once, a wizard fell where clocks met ruin—betrayed, abandoned. Beware his echo, Harlequins, for shadows twist even the truest hearts." Blunt frowned, "Who?" but Mr. Faith turned away, the riddle unfolding.

Hidden in a shadowed archway, the Dark Goblin fumed. "Too easily guided," he sneered. "But soon, your virtues will crumble."

Feeling a sudden chill, Greenie glanced around uneasily. "Did anyone else feel that?"

Firee placed a steady hand on her shoulder. "We're not alone in this quest."

With heartfelt thanks to Mr. Faith, they hastened back to the station. Firee sighed, disappointed. "I hoped we'd find the Orloj right away."

Greenie mustered a smile. "Each step gets us closer."

A Surprise at Wells Cathedral

The **train westward** sped through tranquil fields and villages. By mid-afternoon, they arrived in the small city of Wells. A gentle mist gave the cobblestone streets a mystical glow. The **Gothic towers** of Wells Cathedral soared overhead, intricate stone carvings welcoming them.

Inside, sunlight filtered through stained glass, painting the floor in soft reds and blues. Their attention fixed on the **famous astronomical clock** with miniature knights jousting on the quarter hour.

They expected a standard "arrive, cameo, next clue." But this time, the group found the **main doors blocked** by scaffolding and an apologetic caretaker.

"Repairing old stones," he sighed. "If you want a closer look at the clock, you'll have to enter through the crypt below."

Guided by the caretaker, they descended a narrow staircase into the **cathedral's crypt**. Flickering lanterns revealed damp stone walls and an unexpected gloom. Halfway through, the caretaker vanished—an illusion dissolving into swirling mist.

"Great," Reddish muttered. "A trick?"

A hush fell. Then, from behind a pillar, **Felicia Poindexter** (the Harvard librarian mentor) emerged, wise gaze calm. "Wells's clock requires unity from you. But first, you must face a *mini-challenge*."

Sudden illusions materialized: water rising, threatening to flood the crypt. The Harlequins had to coordinate spells—Checkered and Breezie forming a barrier with conjured air, Reddish and Firee channeling heat to evaporate encroaching water, while Blunt and Greenie kept watch for the hidden exit. The synergy tested them more than any simple riddle.

When the illusions broke, they emerged into the main cathedral, breathless but triumphant. At last, they gathered beneath the clock's face, each feeling the renewed power of *Unity* that Felicia had once taught them. The dials danced a frantic waltz, unveiling a clue in whispers of brass and starlight—a **cryptic reference to Exeter** and its nursery rhyme legends.

"Exeter? Got it! Exeter Cathedral," announced an exicited Firee as he figured out their next stop.

"You have done well," Felicia said quietly. "Remember: not every puzzle is a door…some are a test of your bond."

With that, the caretaker's real shape flickered back into existence. "The cathedral's scaffolding? Sorry, we're repairing centuries' worth of wear," he said with a shrug, clueless about the illusions. Exchanging amused smiles, the Harlequins thanked him and slipped out, newly confident in their synergy.

Exeter Cathedral

Buoyed by success, they took the next train southwest. The lush Somerset fields gave way to Devon's rolling hills, gilded by late-afternoon light. Arriving at Exeter, they sensed an **ancient yet vibrant** magic in the air.

As they stepped into the city of Exeter narrow streets an illusion engulfed them once more…

Past twilight, the Harlequins found themselves in a lonely alley between towering stone facades. Suddenly, **guttural screeches** rent the air—**winged gargoyles** of solidified illusion swooped from the rooftops.

"Incoming!" cried **Greenie**, activating her **energy shield** from Paris. The first gargoyle's claws raked against a shimmering dome. **Reddish** sprang into action, using **spider-climb** to race up the building wall and lob a stun spell from above.

Firee braced with a second shield, while **Checkered** unleashed a clarity blast to reveal the gargoyles' illusory cores. In a swirl of dust, the monstrous forms dissipated. Panting from the brief skirmish, **Blunt** guided them forward. "We need to hurry—these illusions are only stalling us from Exeter."

A few sets ahead they saw it..

Exeter Cathedral's **Norman towers** and imposing stone façade overshadowed the quiet square, ivy trailing from old walls. Inside, soft candlelight danced across high arches. The famed astronomical clock awaited them, but it, too, was motionless.

"Pereunt et imputantur," Checkered read, frowning.

"The hours pass and are reckoned to our account," Firee translated thoughtfully.

They studied the clock, trying to stir its magic. Suddenly, from behind an ornate pillar, stepped **Mrs. Eleanor Peabody-Smith**—the poised antiquarian who had once taught them *Honesty* and *Self-awareness*.

"This clock responds only when you share your truths," she reminded them gently.

Though uneasy, each wizard confessed vulnerabilities, Blunt feared failing those who relied on him, Reddish admitted her boldness could blind her to others' help, Firee confessed that caution sometimes froze him from fully living, Checkered worried her humor hid deeper insecurities, Breezie feared his silence made him seem uncaring, Greenie struggled to trust her intuition.

A gentle hum spread through the cathedral; the clock's dials spun in shimmering alignment. The new clue appeared: **a roaring lion** and **a crescent moon** overshadowed by a cathedral.

"**Norwich**!" Exclaimed an exuberant as the encyclopedic Firee once came through for them.

"My late husband gave me this," Mrs. Peabody-Smith whispered, handing Checkered a **delicate silver charm bracelet**. Her voice trembled. "A reminder that honesty and shared burdens can save you at sea—literal or otherwise."

Grateful, they pressed on, hearts lighter for having faced themselves. Outside, the **Dark Goblin** lurked among the shadows, malevolence emanating. "Virtues!" he spat. "I will delight in shattering them."

Norwich Cathedral

Dusk settled into twilight by the time they reached Norwich. Soft golden streetlamps lit the medieval avenues. The **majestic spire** of Norwich Cathedral rose above half-timbered buildings, an ethereal sight under the evening sky.

A pair of uniformed "cathedral guides" waved them down in a narrow lane. "This way," one insisted, voice too pleasant. **Firee** sensed a twinge of unease, glancing at **Blunt**.

Blunt closed his eyes and invoked **mind-reading**—an ability honed at Prague. Instantly, he glimpsed dark, swirling intent behind the smiling faces. They weren't true guides at all, but illusions set to lead the Harlequins astray into a dead-end.

"They're fakes," he murmured, voice tight. **Reddish** pretended to nod politely to the illusions, then swiftly steered the group down a different passage. Behind them, the false guards melted into shadows. The Harlequins exchanged relieved glances, grateful for the mental skill that kept them on the right path.

Inside, **candles flickered** across polished stone floors. But the cathedral's astronomical clock was ominously still.

"Why isn't it reacting?" Firee murmured.

A resonant voice answered from the shadows: **Mr. Percival Ringwald**, the philosophical mentor. "Norwich demands reflection—not on the clock, but on each other."

Blunt turned to the group. "We must…affirm what we admire in each other?"

They did exactly that, recalling small kindnesses and supportive acts from past adventures. Each compliment awakened deeper camaraderie. The clock rumbled softly, gears spinning with warm, living energy. Its face revealed the **symbols** of Leicester University—a **scholarly figure** and **modern astronomy**—and the impetus to keep learning *Open-Mindedness*.

"Leicester, then," Reddish breathed, half disappointed, half excited.

Mr. Ringwald grinned. "Expand your mind or remain blind to the city's secrets."

From the cloister, the Dark Goblin hissed under his breath. "Their bond deepens... This will not do."

Shivering, Greenie said, "I feel...hostility, like a cold shadow."

"We're not alone," Blunt agreed. "We must remain vigilant."

Steam exhaled as the train rumbled out of Norwich Station, the carriage jostling slightly.

Checkered stretched her legs. "Well, that was something—ghost illusions, knights, scaffolding... I need a nap."

Reddish rubbed her forehead. "Wake me up when illusions start behaving."

Breezie chuckled softly. "You'll be sleeping forever, then."

"Not again—where are Blunt and Reddish?" Firee asked, exasperated.

"Definitely not on the train," Checkered replied, her voice heavy with frustration.

Outside, the countryside blurred past, the rhythmic motion of the train lulling the group into a fragile calm. Yet, the tension never fully left their shoulders.

Back at the station, Blunt and Reddish caught their breath on the platform, the echoes of their narrow escape still fresh.

Blunt exhaled sharply. "We lost the illusions for now. Let's regroup with the others—there's no time to spare."

"Agreed," Reddish nodded. "They'll be near the statue outside… I hope."

They hurried off, hearts pounding, half-expecting the illusions to reappear at any moment.

What's the mystery behind Blunt's disappearing acts? Firee wondered, puzzled.

As if reading his thoughts, Blunt snapped back, "Do you think I want to disappear voluntarily? You better wipe that rictus full of suspicion off your face."

Leicester University

Night draped the cloudy sky by the time they arrived in Leicester. Modern buildings contrasted sharply with the medieval structures they'd seen. Under gentle campus lighting, they located the **Leicester University Astronomical Clock**, a sleek, contemporary masterpiece.

The realization hit them without warning. "Where are Blunt & Greenie?"

A rickety black cab rumbled through cobblestone streets, the driver oblivious to the swirling illusions overhead.

Greenie (glancing out the window at faint runes in the sky): "Those illusions… they're still watching, aren't they?"

Blunt: "Yes, and I suspect they're waiting for the perfect moment to strike."

Rain began to patter, and the cab turned a corner, revealing the silhouette of Leicester's university spire.

Four members of the wizardly bunch sighed in relief as they reunited. Yet, an uneasy, lingering feeling remained—why and how had Blunt and Greenie become separated from the group? *There will be some explaining to do at some point,* thought Firee.

The clock sat still; intricate gears visible beneath a translucent face. Each symbol etched in luminous lines.

"Another silent clock," Breezie noted sadly.

A low chuckle drifted on the breeze. The **Dark Goblin**? Possibly. But from a side corridor emerged **Felicia Poindexter** again, now emphasizing *Innovation and Adaptability*—virtues she had once shared in a lecture to Blunt's father.

"This clock awakens to fresh insights. Reflect on the new ideas you've gained."

They took turns, admitting how they'd grown, Firee recognized that true courage means *accepting help*, Greenie learned her intuition strengthens when shared openly,

Checkered saw that synergy multiplies everyone's talents, Breezie realized empathy can be more potent than force, Reddish found that boldness must be balanced with foresight, Blunt concluded that real leadership means empowering *all*.

The clock pulsed with soft light, gears sliding into motion. Its dials revealed three symbols: an **aircraft** constellation, a **wreath of remembrance**, and the outline of a **towering cathedral**. *York Minster*, they all realized—commemorating WWII airmen.

Felicia gave a gentle laugh. "When I was young, I tried a desert adventure, was hopelessly lost. I learned the greatest leap isn't outward but inward—to adapt, to trust. Remember this as you approach York."

Exchanging thanks, they set off with renewed purpose, though a tingle of dread lingered. The Goblin's presence felt nearby.

York Minster

Twilight's mist cloaked the ancient city of York as they stepped off the train. Each cobblestone street felt older than memory itself. The imposing **York Minster** dominated the skyline, spires stretching toward the stars.

Inside, hush and reverence. A soft glow illuminated the **WWII commemorative clock**, its face etched with constellations once navigated by pilots in the darkest skies. Yet the clock remained still, no cameo or final puzzle emerging.

Disappointed, they turned to leave—until Blunt noticed a seemingly humble **maintenance worker** at the door, gaze oddly intense. Realization struck.

"Kraus!" Checkered whispered.

Kraus smiled faintly, acknowledging them all. "You seek the Orloj, but it's not here. Not exactly." He gestured toward the clock's shimmering face. "True bravery lies in remembering those who sacrificed. Their legacy lights your path. You have shown respect for that legacy—thus, the Orloj acknowledges you."

The clock face glowed with **celestial brilliance**, its constellation forming **Big Ben's iconic shape**.

"Big Ben," Reddish murmured, eyes shining with awe.

Kraus nodded gently. "Exactly. The real Orloj is woven into London's hidden heartbeat—inside Big Ben itself. Now that you've proved your readiness, the way into *parallel London* stands open."

With a swirl of magic, he guided them to an alcove near the cathedral entrance. Air shimmered, forming a **portal** of swirling lights.

Antonella and Bart stood back, **hands clasped** as the swirl of magical energy began to thicken in the air. Neither could hide the flicker of **protective urgency** in their eyes. This portal crossing was well beyond ordinary travel, and it never stopped **worrying** them—even if they had seen glimpses of it before.

"We'll wait for you in London," Bart repeated, his voice stronger than his trembling fingers. "No matter what happens, remember how proud we are."

Antonella's eyes shone with **a fierce but unspoken love** for her nephew and his friends. She managed a brave smile. "Come back safe, all of you. We're with you every step—even if we can't physically follow."

The six exchanged determined looks. **Firee offered a quick wave**, Reddish grinned reassuringly, and Blunt gave a short salute. Then, with final nods of trust, they stepped into the portal. Reality **blurred** around them, the station's noise and the anxious gazes of Bart and Antonella fading into swirling colors—**a final image of parental devotion** lingering as they vanished.

Moments later, they found themselves surrounded by Big Ben's **massive gears**, the clockwork ticking like a heartbeat.

Their final quest had begun.

Chapter 3

Under the Shadow of Big Ben

A surreal stillness surrounded the group as they found themselves inside the intricate, towering mechanism of Big Ben. Massive gears, pendulums, and clock hands loomed around them, ticking with a rhythm that resonated deep within their bones. Yet beneath that audible ticking, there was a subtler *hum*—a constant vibration that no ordinary human ear could sense—one that whispered of powerful magic awakened here.

They stood in awe, breaths misting slightly in the cool, metallic air.

"We're actually inside Big Ben," Breezie whispered, eyes wide in wonder. "It's incredible."

Checkered peered around, her gaze restless. "But if this is Big Ben, then where is the Orloj we've been seeking?"

Almost in response, a deep, melodic chime reverberated through the space, a vibration that hummed through air and floor and their very bodies. The immense gears slowed, then halted. A swirl of golden mist drifted down gracefully from above, revealing the **translucent face of a celestial clock**—glowing vividly with symbols of stars, planets, moons, and suns. It hovered majestically, rotating gently as though inviting them closer.

"The Orloj…" Blunt said reverently, stepping forward.

"No," came a soft yet firm voice. The group turned sharply to see a slender, silver-haired boy emerge from the shadows. His movements were impossibly fluid, each step placed with uncanny grace. "I am **Chronos**, Keeper and Confidant of the Orloj. You stand at the gateway of your final trial."

Chronos paused, his gaze distant. "Time mourns its lost keepers—those who faltered, left to crumble in towers of their own making."

Greenie tilted her head, but the Orloj's chime drowned her question.

When it subsided **Greenie** asked. "You're the Keeper of the Orloj? But what do you keep?"

Chronos offered a faint smile. "Balance," he said, as though it were the simplest answer in the world. "I ensure time's flow remains true, especially when illusions threaten it."

He paused at the faint shimmer of another gear's hum. "The Orloj itself keeps something far more challenging: **all of you.**"

A quiet amazement stole over them. **Breezie** opened his mouth to question further, but Chronos raised a hand gently, guiding them along a narrow corridor of rotating gears. Shadows danced across the metal surfaces, the subdued hum still tickling their senses.

"Come," Chronos urged, gesturing to a softly glowing square of mist.

"We must not waste a moment. The Orloj's final test—your *24 hours*—began the instant its chime welcomed you. Time here has *its own pulse*, and you'll need every moment it grants."

At the mention of "24 hours," **Reddish** exchanged a tense glance with Firee. They all sensed the weight of a countdown, though no ordinary clock displayed it.

Thumbpee and **Buggie** fluttered in the background, offering no explanation—only watchful presence. As the young wizards crossed into the swirling portal, reality dissolved around them, colors bleeding like ink in water. Each heartbeat stretched, each breath felt elongated and dreamlike.

With a gentle *snap*, the world reformed—sharp, immediate, breathtaking. They landed on ancient cobblestones worn smooth by centuries of footsteps. A luminous twilight blanketed the city in hues of amethyst and indigo, casting dreamlike shadows that flickered and danced.

They were still in **London**, but not the one they had known. Familiar landmarks rose around them, yet each glowed with enchanted grandeur. **Big Ben** towered overhead, its face softly radiant, pulsing gently like a massive heartbeat, encircled by drifting clockwork gears that glimmered in midair. Streetlamps sang with invisible harps, their glow pulsing over cobblestones damp with lavender mist. A vendor's cart clattered, spilling thyme-scented sparks into the dusk.

The streets bustled with life unlike anything imaginable: witches in embroidered cloaks traded glowing herbs, wizards in velvet robes conjured illusions of dragonfire, enchanted mirrors winked from shop windows. Every stone, every breath, *thrummed* with magic.

Firee inhaled the air, tingling with energy. "Parallel London…"

"Yes." **Breezie** looked up at the swirling lights that formed invisible ley lines across the night sky. "We've truly crossed over."

Suddenly, the enormous clock face above them glowed fiercely, its hands spinning before settling on midnight. The Orloj thundered to life, its voice a storm of gears and grace, calling them forth like pilgrims to a timeless shrine:

"Welcome, young wizards!"

They gasped, recognizing the presence that had guided them in other Orloj quests. The voice crackled with fatherly warmth, each syllable echoing with ancient authority. **The Orloj** was speaking to them directly, woven into the fabric of this parallel city.

"You have journeyed far, learned deeply, and proven yourselves worthy thus far.

Now you stand in **Parallel London**, a realm of wonder and peril—shaped by your strengths and weaknesses. Here, the shadows you've sensed will take form to challenge you."

A chill ran down **Checkered's** spine. "We've felt that darkness following us… The Dark Goblin."

Orloj's tone grew solemn. "Yes. He hungers for your missteps—any unmastered flaw will be his advantage. Recall the virtues you've gathered. Overconfidence or neglect will cost you dearly."

Greenie swallowed, eyes flicking around at the mesmerizing city. "And…if we manage to endure these next trials?"

The Orloj's clock face pulsed. "In *24 short hours*, if your virtues shine undimmed, you shall ascend beyond Master Wizards—becoming **Orloj Wizards**, guardians of virtue and balance. But heed this: illusions run deeper here. Trust your friends, or your powers may vanish at the worst moment."

A hush settled. The group exchanged determined looks. **Reddish** breathed, "24 hours to prove we can do this. Let's not fail now."

"There is more," Orloj continued gently, "your mentors will appear in disguises—test your wits to recognize them. You cannot read their thoughts here. Only by living each virtue will you conquer the illusions to come."

A final pulse of brilliant light rippled from Big Ben's face, revealing a **shimmering portal** nearby.

"Step forward," Orloj commanded. "Time is fleeting—your final quest has begun."

At the edge of their vision, hidden in the labyrinth of floating gears, a twisted form crouched, eyes gleaming with malevolent joy: **the Dark Goblin** at last, poised to spring its trap. It had lurked on the threshold of their journey, patient and voracious, waiting for the moment they let their guard down. Now, with the portal open and the young wizards taking their first steps into **the Orloj's final trial**, the Goblin felt a surge of triumph.

A low hiss escaped its throat. **Where virtue faltered, it would feast on fear and doubt.** Determination or not, these children had only twenty-four hours to face illusions beyond imagination—and the Goblin would ensure those illusions struck deep.

Beyond the swirling gateway, **Blunt** and his friends squared their shoulders, hearts pounding with anticipation. They could not yet sense the Goblin's claws at their backs, nor could they guess how fiercely darkness would contest their every virtue. But their resolve stood unshaken as they stepped forward into the shimmering portal, fully intent on conquering the trials within.

Thus, in the electrified hush of Parallel London's clockwork streets, the ultimate challenge began.

Chapter 4

First Tower Illusion

Nightfall had transformed Parallel London into a captivating metropolis of magic. Floating lanterns drifted lazily above cobbled roads, while wizards in sumptuous cloaks conjured subtle illusions for passing crowds. Shop signs flickered with runic characters, promising potions and spells unknown to mortal eyes. Despite the enchantment, the **Harlequins** felt an undercurrent of tension—**something** lurked in the shadows, feeding on their every uncertainty.

At the **Tower of London**, clouds tinted purple, and gold glimmered across ancient ramparts. But beneath the regal facade, an **invisible chill** lingered. The **Dark Goblin** watched, unseen, waiting for these young wizards to falter in *virtue* so he could strike.

Illusions on the Thames

The group navigated the dimly lit alleys near the Tower, harlequin suits casting a gentle glow. Suddenly, raucous laughter erupted from a hidden side street. A band of street performers—fiery jugglers, swirling ribbons of light—spilled into the thoroughfare, corralling the Harlequins in a chaotic circle.

"Careful," **Blunt** warned, eyes flicking warily between illusions.

Before they could retreat, one flamboyant magician snapped his fingers. **Checkered** felt an invisible jerk on her cloak, and all six Harlequins found themselves suspended over the **black, churning Thames**. The conjurer cackled as the illusions released them, sending them plummeting.

"Use Clarity's Lens!" **Firee** shouted.

With practiced speed, **Blunt** activated the lens they had earned from a prior mentor. At once, **glowing threads** of magic became visible around them. **Checkered** pointed out a stable strand, and the Harlequins latched onto it mid-fall. The illusions guided them onto a small, illusory barge below—a precarious but lifesaving landing.

Greenie trembled at the railing, gazing into dark waters. "I'm afraid my instincts might fail us," she admitted softly.

Firee gave her shoulder a comforting squeeze. "They haven't yet—and if you stumble, we'll help you."

The Haunting Tune

As the barge plunged, Reddish's vision swam—Barcelona's sunlit plaza, her family's stern faces. "Your reckless magic shames us," her mother hissed, turning away. Her brother's sneer burned: "You're no daughter of ours." **Reddish's** chest tightened, her boldness faltering.

The Thames roared, the air tasted of salt and old oak, the barge creaking like a ship adrift in time. It shimmered with ghostly oarsmen in ruffled collars, humming a forgotten Elizabethan shanty, their voices threading magic into the river's pulse.

But **Reddish** saw their pride slipping like sand. "I fight for your pride, not mine," she murmured, voice soft against the wind. The illusion faded as The Busker's hand steadied her, his eyes kind. "Generosity gives what pride hoards," he said.

They disembarked onto a quiet courtyard near the Tower's walls. Then, a **mournful melody** tugged at their hearts—a lover's tune, laced with gentle magic. Londoners bustled past the musician as though he were invisible, their eyes vacant, indifferent. But the Harlequins *felt* each chord like a subtle plea.

"How is nobody noticing this?" **Reddish** asked, brow furrowing.

Checkered frowned. "Sometimes people ignore what doesn't concern them—like they can't spare empathy."

The Busker caught **Blunt**'s eye, an ancient spark flashing across his face, then darted into a winding alley. The Harlequins followed, hearts pounding with curiosity. They soon hit a **dead-end**: a solid brick wall.

An instant later, the **stones rippled** like water, forming a door with glowing golden letters:

"Antique Books for The Spirit and The Soul"

(Est. long, long time ago)

The door swung open. The Busker, now revealed as **Cornelius Tetragor** in regal attire—long white hair, kind eyes—beckoned them in. "Welcome, Harlequins. You found me."

Cornelius Tetragor emerged, a silhouette of kindness carved from light, his smile a lantern against the Thames's shadowed tide. He lifted the edges of his long, cream-colored robe, revealing how easily the flowing fabric trailed behind him. His long white hair, bound in a neat ponytail at his nape, swayed gently with every measured step. Despite his serene smile, a quiet intensity played in his keen eyes, as though he could peer straight into unspoken truths.

"Generosity," he remarked in a sonorous voice, "is the simplest virtue, yet the hardest to live. Even illusions are undone by those who speak plainly to themselves."

He turned his ponytailed head sharply toward Blunt, adding, "Come, dear wizards. A Generous mind seldom stumbles in the dark." Then, with a subtle gesture, he guided them deeper into the shop, the folds of his robe trailing like a ripple of ivory light.

Inside the Antique Bookstore

They stepped through into a **towering library** of floating shelves and softly glowing orbs. Dust motes shimmered in the lamplight, and the hush of old tomes enveloped them. Cornelius closed the door, speaking gently:

"You were tested tonight by illusions that prey on *indifference*. You saw how crowds ignored the Busker, how conjurers attacked you for sport. Such apathy can be more dangerous than malice. Most of the time we underestimate others, guided by our emotions, the busker others ignored, appreciated your interest on him and his craft," Cornelius said. "He noticed you. And is thankful for your interest. Here is a small gesture he has gifted you," Tetragor added.

*

"The Magical City Busker"

Through winding streets, where echoes play,
A childlike spirit lights the way.
Always smiling, boundless heart,
Sharing art in every part.

He calls himself a busker true,
A private performer just for you.
His songs create collective cheer,
A little boy who holds us near.

From a "Sky Full of Stars" above,

He tries to "Fix Us" with his love.

Sometimes a "Scientist" in thought,

With melodies that heal and teach what can't be taught.

He reminds us "Clocks" are ticking still,

And urges us to "Pray" with will.

He pleads with us to "Vivir la Vida",

To fuel our passions with Reds and "Yellows" of fire,

To love, to dance, to dream, to feel.

He warns that "Every Teardrop Is a Waterfall",

Yet shows us there's "Paradise" for all.

Inviting us to "His Universe",

A place where hope and wonder burst.

Sometimes he just desires to "Talk",

To share a moment on life's walk.

He pleads for us not to "Shiver",

And whispers softly, "Don't Panic", be a giver.

Avoiding paths that lead to "Trouble's" door,

He guides us toward adventures more.

He beckons us to take the ride,

To live life fully, "At the Speed of Light".

He sings of dreams both bold and bright,

A call to hearts lost in the night.

He invites us all to chase the climb,

To join him on "The Adventure of a Lifetime."

Grateful always, inspired still,

He spreads his music, heart and will.

A troubadour without a stage,

His life, a song, a living page.

*

"He is a true-life wizard," Cornelius added. He then guided them into a cozy reading nook, plush chairs arranged in a circle. "To break indifference, you must embrace **Generosity**," explained Cornelius with soft words filled with wisdom. From a worn tome, he earnestly began to read:

*

"Flowers From the Heart"

Small flower arrangements, predominantly roses, show up every morning at each one of the doorsteps of the small suburban community.

Except for the child and his grandma eavesdropping at sunrise, from the Red Victorian house attic, no one else knows who brings the flowers no one is asked to pay for them either.

Yet, they never fail to be, neither to paint bright smiles of joy, as well as happy hearts and chuckles from the fortunate flower recipients.

As he does each and every morning, the humble, wandering man, places flower arrangements right at every doorstep; beautifully red roses prepared and cut with love and tender care.

The man delivering flowers from the heart, lives without a roof over his head; He is disheveled, wears ragged clothes, and noisy, cracked shoes; his bushy hair and beard are tangled and dusty, his strides are bouncy and wayward, yet somehow, they always take him to his intended destination.

"How does he do it?" Asks Jenny, her youngest granddaughter.

"Nobody knows, he is homeless man," replies in amazement Grannie, "One thing I know is that he cannot afford it," Grannie adds.

His big secret is actually no such thing; the secrets of the heart are not hard to fathom if one just looks close enough, but only through the lenses of our own genuine love and affection.

The homeless man rummages and scrabs as he always does, but for the case of his daily offerings, he does it through all of the neighboring town's flower shops dumpsters. There he finds an abundance of discarded flowers, enough to fulfill his purpose and daily good deeds.

"*Granny, can you see the kind of shoes he wears?*"

Jenny asks with shock on her voice.

"*Not quite, dear, only that they are quite noisy as he drags them through the floor, what kind of shoes is the homeless man wearing?*" *Granny asks puzzled.*

"*Granny, Granny, he's wearing baseball shoes, the homeless man is walking on cleats the whole day long,*" *says and exalted and teary-eyed Jenny.*

"*What a terrible thing for such a good man,*" *observes Granny realizing how cumbersome it must be for the homeless man.*

"*What should we do Granny, we have to do something!*" *Jenny says.*

"*I don't know dear, why should we change anything?*

Sometimes giving involves great sacrifices; on the other hand, most of the times we don't appreciate or value what is behind and what does it take for us to receive some of the most wonderful gifts we enjoy," *reflects Granny in an open-ended fashion.*

Impromptu, all of the sudden, the young child pulls her grandmother into a small store.

All excited Jenny asks, chooses, and buys the most comfortable shoes the store offers.

Then she runs after the homeless man and offers him the shoes.

He seems flustered and indecisive, while the young child places the shoes on his hands and runs away immediately back to Granny.

The good man hesitates for a while until he sits down on a bench and tries the shoes and walks a few steps.

His head then turns around slowly, until he meets the young child eyes.

The homeless man then flashes the brightest and widest of all smiles, and the Young girl smiles back at him trembling with joy and tears.

The homeless man then walks away.

He still has his daily mission to accomplish, but the homeless man knows and is happy about it, that he is now much better prepared to accomplish it.

*

He closed the book softly. The Harlequins sat in thoughtful silence.

Reddish broke the hush. "He gave flowers to everyone without asking for anything. That's generosity—but it began with his caring heart."

Breezie added, "And then the girl showed generosity in return, helping him with shoes. She *saw* his struggle and acted."

Cornelius nodded. "A perfect example of **Generosity**. One caring deed seed another. Indifference would have let him suffer unnoticed."

Testing Their Understanding

A faint shimmer in the store's far corner drew their attention: a **ghostly child** in ragged clothes, tearful eyes brimming with sorrow. She reached out silently, as illusions of passersby parted around her, indifferent.

The Harlequins acted **together**—not just to dispel the illusion but to comfort the child. **Checkered** conjured a small orb of warmth, **Firee** offered gentle light, and **Greenie** whispered reassuring words. The child flickered, then dissolved into a soft glow of gratitude.

"You *chose* **Generosity**, showing compassion over apathy," Cornelius observed. "That's how you face illusions born from indifference."

He shut both tomes, returning them to the shelves. "I once hoarded knowledge, ignoring everyone's needs," he confessed. "A young apprentice's kindness wrenched me from my solitude. Since then, I've championed these virtues."

A Glowing Lens

They followed Cornelius back outside. The door clicked shut behind them. As they stepped from the bookstore's glow, the Tower's stones blurred into swirling mist, depositing them beneath a moonlit corner of Parallel London's timeless streets.

When they turned around, the **entire bookstore façade vanished**—just a blank, old wall. In its place, a **small lens** hovered, gleaming in midair.

Blunt carefully cupped it. At once, a gentle echo of Cornelius's voice resounded in their thoughts:

"When illusions blind you and indifference tempts your heart, let *Kindness* ignite your *Generosity*. Then, no darkness shall prevail."

Firee recognized it with excitement. "Another form of *Clarity's Lens*, keyed to reveal not just illusions, but any heartlessness or apathy!"

Checkered exhaled, tucking the lens safely. "We'll need it."

Dark Goblin's Frustration

Within the **deepest** Tower shadows, the **Dark Goblin** seethed. Rage and cunning flickered across his twisted features. He sensed the Harlequins' bond growing even stronger. But his lips curved into a cruel grin; he had countless illusions still to unleash.

Renewed Resolve

Stepping away from the now-empty courtyard, the Harlequins felt a swell of purpose. They had stared **indifference** in the face—and refused it. Strengthened by lessons of **Kindness** fueling **Generosity**, they pressed on into Parallel London's magical night.

The city was far from safe, illusions ready to ensnare them at every turn. Yet they knew apathy was the Goblin's easiest victory. As long as they *acted* with compassion, remembering the homeless man's daily sacrifice or the tearful child illusions, they would not fail. The next trial lay ahead, but they were prepared to **see** and **care**—to choose empathy where others might turn away.

And so it ended, the **antique bookstore** gone without a trace, leaving only the luminous lens and a deeper resolve in each Harlequin's heart. **They would not be indifferent** to any cry for help—nor to any illusions cast by the Goblin—ever again.

Chapter 5

Lost in the Labyrinth

Morning rose softly over the rooftops of Parallel London, yet the six Harlequins felt little comfort from the gentle dawn. Anxiety weighed on them, each painfully aware that precious hours had slipped by in a **magical labyrinth** twisting London's streets into something unrecognizable. They had found no sign of the next mentor, and frustration gnawed at their spirits.

"We've passed this corner three times," **Greenie** said, annoyance clear as she stared at an oddly mirrored shop window filled with levitating trinkets.

They stood at a busy crossroads, bustling with wizards and conjurers going about their business. Yet each lane looked eerily similar, illusions shifting building facades and signboards. **Checkered** exhaled softly, noticing a faded hourglass image on an old stone wall—a silent reminder that *time* was against them.

"Are we growing wiser, or just racing in circles?" she murmured, tracing the hourglass with a fingertip.

Blunt offered a small smile. "Wisdom isn't always obvious in the moment. Every choice—right or wrong—teaches us something."

Breezie nodded; gaze distant. "And each grain of sand that falls shapes who we're becoming."

Still, their progress felt futile. **Hours** of wandering brought no mentor, no clue. **Breezie** finally sighed, voice edged with fatigue: "It's nearly dawn, and we're stuck. No sign of our next guide."

A Bewitching Distraction

Just then, distant orchestral music drifted through the early morning haze. Following the sound, they emerged onto a broad square filled with **Victorian-dressed revelers** dancing around sparkling fountains. At first, it seemed enchanting—but **Firee** sensed a subtle menace beneath the merriment.

"It could be another illusion," he warned. "We can't afford more distractions."

Too late—a swirl of dancers surrounded them, vibrant costumes spinning in dizzying arcs. The Harlequins found themselves **caught** in a spell that forced them to join the dance.

Blunt shouted over the rising music, "Use Clarity's Lens—now!"

At once, the lens's familiar glow cut through the illusions. **Breezie** pinpointed an **escape route**, gesturing decisively. Together, they **broke free**, slipping away breathless into a side street. The illusions vanished, leaving them in an **unfamiliar** district, far from where they'd started.

The Harlequins found modern city lights mingling with stray magical lanterns.

Firee (running a hand through his hair): "Feels like two worlds meshed—tech and illusions."

Checkered: "We better find our next mentor and their traveling antique books store, soon. Keep your eyes open for any sign."

The group headed into bustling streets, scanning each building for the glint of arcane power.

Panting, **Checkered** groaned. "We wasted more time—again. If only we'd used the lens sooner…"

Regrouping and a Child's Sob

At last, the Harlequins stumbled onto a small square under a flickering lamppost, hearts pounding from the chase. **Thumbpee** perched irritably on Blunt's shoulder, delivering a sharp admonishment.

"You had Clarity's Lens all along! Why chase illusions blindly? If you keep letting confusion reign, you'll lose your gifts."

Though they protested softly—didn't they *use* the lens? — Thumbpee's scolding reminder stung. He was right: **discipline** meant using their powers preemptively, not just in crisis.

Before they could argue further, **Buggie** buzzed overhead, shining a tiny green beam onto a dim alley. **Checkered** squinted, "Our mentor might be *there*?"

Thumbpee folded his arms. "Possibly. Remember, you must practice your virtues constantly. Panic, carelessness—these let illusions thrive."

Steeling themselves, **Blunt** raised the lens once more, focusing both outward and inward. A new clarity settled over them, revealing a path that glowed subtly in rhythm with their heartbeats. They followed it, determined not to be fooled again.

Suddenly, a soft **sobbing** echoed from a cramped side lane. The Harlequins hesitated —time was short. But **Checkered** resolutely shook her head. "Kindness is never a distraction," she murmured. Reluctantly, the others joined her.

They found a small child clutching a **shattered porcelain doll**, tears rolling unnoticed by the passing illusions. **Greenie** knelt beside her gently. "What happened?"

"My doll…it's broken," the girl sniffled.

Without waiting, **Firee** gathered the pieces and cast a **tender** mending charm. The doll reassembled as though brand new. The child gasped, eyes shining with gratitude, then melted away into the city's illusions as if she'd never been there.

Kindness Reveals the Mentor

A resonant voice spoke from the shadows: **Lazarus Zeetrikus**, stepped forward. His presence radiated both gravity and warmth.

"You found me at last. Only an act of kindness—helping a stranger with no thought of reward—could lead you here."

Lazarus Zeetrikus stood taller than any Harlequin present. His old bent hat wobbled precariously atop his shock of coarse white hair, giving him a slightly whimsical air. But the gravity in his lined face suggested deeper pains. Sometimes, his lips pressed together as though warring with lingering bitterness. Despite this, he offered them a gentle half-bow. "I was known for nursing grudges," he said gravely, tapping the bent brim of his hat. "But grudges only weigh you down, children. Kindness dissolves them faster than time."

Lazarus inhaled, the tall frame swaying beneath the weight of old regrets. "I once refused to forgive a friend," he confessed, voice trembling, "and illusions devoured me for it. Don't let them seize your heart the same way."

He gestured for them to follow, guiding them through winding alleys until they reached a **nearly invisible wooden door** tucked between decrepit buildings. Golden letters glimmered:

"The Jester, Antique Books for All Ages"

(Est. long, long time ago)

Inside, the bookstore was hushed and **magical**: shelves stacked sky-high, floating lanterns illuminating tomes bound in exotic materials. Lazarus took a seat by an ornate lectern, inviting the Harlequins to gather round.

First, he opened a slim volume and earnestly with a serene cadence of soft words filled with wisdom began to read:

*

"Kindness"

It's the genuine, spontaneous,
humble, and giving gesture.

It's gentle and noble generosity,
It's pious empathy,
It's classy humbleness,
and candor of the heart.

It's uninterested charm,
A rare virtue that does not seek,
expects or needs a reward.

It's pure love drenched in respect;

It's egoless acts without accolades,

the well-intentioned deed,

the free-willing, profoundly wise choice,

where our best attributes and our life's clock,

-driven by the purest forms of love,

and steered by sheer empathy-

are put to good use

for the well-being or betterment of others.

Kindness is a heavenly gift

that is hard to find or give space to

in "the big scheme of things,"

yet it abounds in spades,

and takes place

in the little moments,

in the tiny, bitty details in life,

that's where it resides,

that's where it can be found.

Authentic Kindness,

one of the truest, most precious treasures,

we can dote on or put to good use in life.

*

He closed the book gently, letting the words sink in. "Kindness is never wasted effort, nor is it weakness," Lazarus said quietly. "It transforms hearts—like yours did with that weeping child."

Next, he retrieved another old manuscript, labeled with swirling script, and continued to read with gusto:

*

"The Street Vendor From Portoviejo"

The youngster walks the streets of Portoviejo;
He peddles incessantly,
without a permit,
from sunrise to sundown.

Every day,
early in the morning,
he takes the bus to the city center,
that's where he remains for the rest of the day.

Chestnut unruly hair mops his forehead,
his eyes always looking startled and in awe,
the youngster wears wrinkled short pants,
checkered canvas sneakers,
and the white and diagonal red stripe t-shirt
of the Peruvian National Soccer Team.

The spirited youngster whistles and hums all day long,

always carried by a cheerful spirit,
a steely resolve,
and a sunny disposition
drenched with enthusiasm
towards life and its people.

As long as he can carry the load
throughout the day,
the street vendor normally offers
the kind of products his customers want.

He has an innate pulse for the market,
that's why he's seldom wrong,
when he chooses what to sell each day.

What he offers today
seem like ragged strands of cloth and leather,
hanging from both sides of his forearms.

Upon closer examination,
what he showcases,
are belts and ties.

But his trade is not free of hiccups.
His main concern

is to stay one step ahead of the police,
otherwise, his goods would be immediately confiscated.

He knows the authorities normally look the other way
at what he does.
Yet, one never knows what kind of law enforcement agent
will show up on any particular day...?

His constant fear is not to be robbed
either by his potential clients,
or street criminals
which unfortunately abound
on the city streets.

"There are no better ties and Belts in the market;
I've got them in all sizes and colors, pick one,
two or three and this could be the day
that good fortune smiles at you!"
He peddles incessantly.

Walking by a street café,
unsolicited,
the street vendor approaches a table
where a heavy-set man, and an attractive woman
dine outdoors.

Approaching the side of the table
where the inattentive man sits,
the animated youngster displays his belts and ties
by lifting one arm, and then the other.

Initially the heavy-set man ignores the youngster,
but when the effusive street vendor insists,
the man angrily waves him off,
and when the persistent youngster tries again,
the heavyset man explodes.

He stands up yelling, cursing and screaming
at the shocked, and scared street peddler.

"Don't you know how to respect people's privacy?"
"Give me one of those," the heavyset man says,
unexpectedly yanking one of the belts
from the youngster's arm.
"This is just trash," he says,
and without even inspecting it,
violently throws the belt to the floor.
"Now, get the hell out of here,"
the angry man yells,
ignoring his female companion lecturing complains.

Dejected the young street vendor
hastily picks up the belt,
and walks hurriedly across the street
where he sits on a bus stop bench.
He looks dejected,
his back hunched and his head down.

At the table the heavy-set man
dines with gusto,
until... suddenly, he doesn't.

Right after swallowing
a handful of peanuts
at first, he coughs,
then he begins to choke.

While his companion seems totally helpless,
in a hasty almost violent move,
the heavy-set man jumps into a standing position,
frantically flapping his arms
the angry man is unable to breathe.

Across the street the youngster salesman
notices the commotion,

and without thinking runs towards

the choking heavy-set man.

From behind the afflicted man's back

the young street salesman

slides both his arms underneath the armpits

and around the choking man's chest.

But when he tries to lift him up

while applying pressure

to the afflicted man's chest,

the youngster simply cannot do it.

The desperate man is simply too large and heavy.

Undeterred, the youngster releases its grip,

quickly picks-up one of his belts,

and again from behind the choking man's back

this time he slides the belt around the man's chest.

By pulling both ends of the belt from the back,

The youngster tightens the belt's grip applying pressure

to the man's chest.

The jerky —yet continuous—

tightening and release movements

—also known as the Heimlich maneuver—
seeks to create on the choking man,
an urge to throw up.

And so it happens,
The heavy-set man coughs out a piece of something
that was choking him.
To the angry man immediate relief,
when it flies out of his mouth unannounced,
magic happens,
the life-death moment vanishes in an instant.

When his focus and attention returns,
the heavy-set man realizes
that the young street vendor
has in all probably just saved his life.

His expression changes from relief
to embarrassment, then tears of shame,
he walks slowly towards his unlikely savior
with an expression of deep gratitude.

He embraces the youngster tightly
and begins to sob profusely,
finally releasing all the bottled stress and fear

he accumulated while in distress.

"Thank You So Much Miracle Worker,
I did and do not deserve
your good deed, generosity or mercy."

The heavy-set man then sees,
all the youngster's belts and ties
spread out and lying on the floor,
without hesitation,
he picks up one by one,
and once organized,
hands them to the young street vendor.

While doing so, the heavy-set man
vows his head in a sign
of absolute respect
to his generous savior.

"You had the integrity and strength of character,
to put aside on an instant,
resentment and grudges,
replacing them
with courage and genuine kindness,
both key ingredients of a giving heart,"

It is a life lesson with which you've have blessed me,
One I will treasure, forever more.

*

Lazarus finished reading, letting silence linger. Then he asked, "What do you see in that story?"

Breezie was the first to speak. "The peddler was humiliated and could've walked away—but he chose kindness. He saved someone who wronged him."

Checkered added softly, "It's more than just politeness—it's a readiness to help, even when you've been hurt."

Shanghai's alleys flickered—Breezie, younger, brushing past a beggar's outstretched hand. "Spare a coin?" the man rasped, but **Breezie** hurried on. Later, his still form haunted the street, dead. "I didn't see," **Breezie** whispered now, shame curling in his gut. Lazarus's voice was gentle, "Kindness notices." The illusion faded, leaving **Breezie** trembling.

Lazarus inclined his head, satisfied. "Yes. True kindness *forgets* grudges, enabling compassion in the face of hostility. Indifference or resentment would have let that man choke. But kindness transcended it."

Gifts of the Heart

As Lazarus closed the book, the store's lamplight flickered in a swirl of gentle magic. He turned to Blunt, offering a folded parchment. "Take this. It reveals a new power: **Empath's**

Sight. With it, you can glimpse the *emotions* behind illusions, seeing truth beyond the masks."

Reddish, meanwhile, noticed another small parchment on a nearby shelf. It shimmered softly, letters rearranging:

"Heart's Shield"

Breezie read it with growing excitement. "A protective barrier for our feelings. It can fend off emotional attacks from illusions—especially the Dark Goblin's manipulations."

Lazarus smiled. "Precisely. You have shown kindness, and it grants you empathy. Nurture it well. There's no time to lose."

Greenie hesitated, recalling her earlier doubts. "But—what about the mistakes we made? Are we truly ready?"

Lazarus's intense gaze softened. "Kindness doesn't require perfection. It requires sincerity. Each act deepens your strength. Remember the child with her broken doll, the peddler who saved a cruel man's life—kindness always leaves room to grow."

With that, he faded gently into the shadows, bookstore shelves and lanterns dissolving around them. The building vanished, leaving the Harlequins on a quiet street under the warming sky.

A Final Urgency

Clutching **Empath's Sight** and **Heart's Shield**, the Harlequins stepped back into Parallel London's dawn. Already, the illusions and swirling energies had shifted, the city's layout morphing yet again. They glanced at each other, aware of **the looming clock** on their progress: only so many hours left.

Thumbpee hovered crossly, but his voice held a note of approval. "At least you found the right mentor this time. Now, use these gifts wisely—Time. Is. Short."

A tremor of unease ran through the group. From the far end of the alley, the **Dark Goblin** peered at them with cold delight. They couldn't see him, but they felt his malevolent presence, hungry to exploit any slip.

Still, they stood stronger now, emboldened by the virtue of **Kindness**: an empathy that overcame grudges, a willingness to help even in adversity. A subtle glow emanated from the new powers in their hands—**Empath's Sight** and **Heart's Shield**—ready to repel illusions that toyed with their emotions.

Exchanging determined nods, they stepped forward. Next clue or not, they would continue on with hearts unguarded by bitterness—*but protected* by compassion. Another trial awaited, but with **Kindness** fueling every step, they would not walk in fear.

Narrow alleyways twisted in endless loops of color. Each turn revealed more illusions snarling with the Goblin's laughter. **Firee** spotted a clearing, but illusions blocked every path.

"We can't fight them all," **Greenie** said, voice taut. "But— remember our portal power from Prague?"

Breezie nodded, "Only works if we *all* agree on the destination!"

Illusions lunged, shadows writhing overhead. Rapidly, the six Harlequins locked eyes in silent consensus: "The nearest open square by the Jester's Shop." **Blunt** swiped his hand through the air. A shimmering door appeared, warping light around it. With a collective burst of will, they stepped through—vanishing mere seconds before illusions collapsed onto the spot. They reemerged into calm sunlight, still panting, but free.

Suspicion Grows

Greenie (clutching Empath's Sight): "Did anyone else sense… betrayal in that last illusion? Like the Goblin was testing our trust?"

Firee (eyes grim): "He's done more than test it. He's craving our slip-ups."

Lightning flickered overhead, casting jagged shadows on the rooftops.

Blunt: "We'll move on, but let's not ignore the signs. The worst may still lie ahead."

They turned the corner, illusions swirling in the distance, promising anything but rest.

Chapter 6

Breakfast with the Orloj

Dawn cast its first golden rays over **Parallel London**, dispelling the last vestiges of night's enchantment. Streets once aglow with nocturnal magic stirred anew—wizards purchased fresh potion ingredients at lively stalls, small children on broomsticks giggled as they practiced low-hovering spells, and elegant carriages drawn by winged horses clip-clopped along cobblestones. The city thrummed with bright, radiant energy.

For the **Harlequins**, however, the new day brought mounting urgency. They had spent precious hours fending off illusions, narrowly escaping traps. They knew each moment mattered; the Orloj's ticking clock overshadowed their final quest.

A Surprising Breakfast Invitation

As they navigated toward **Big Ben**, a jovial, booming voice called out:

"Harlequins! Over here!"

Startled, they spotted a **burly man** seated at a cozy street café. Recognition flickered across **Blunt**'s face: "Orloj!"

Exchanging excited looks, they hurried over. Indeed, **the Orloj**—in human guise—sat with an easy grin, **Buggie** flitting overhead and **Thumbpee** perched sternly by a sugar bowl. The surrounding café bustled with robed wizards sipping aromatic teas, a few levitating pastries absentmindedly while engrossed in conversation.

"Come," the Orloj said warmly, gesturing to spare chairs. "Share a meal with me. We've much to discuss."

They settled in. Servers brought **enchanted pastries** that subtly glowed with runic designs, pots of tea steaming gently. For a brief moment, they allowed themselves to feel the city's morning optimism.

Reviewing Their Progress

Between bites, the Orloj's eyes—kind yet penetrating—swept over each Harlequin. "You've done well, but I sense you've struggled. The **Dark Goblin** grows bolder, feeding on your indecision."

Firee swallowed nervously, setting down his cup. "He keeps catching us unprepared. We have these powers—Clarity's Lens, Heart's Shield—but we sometimes forget to use them until it's nearly too late."

A flicker of fatherly disapproval crossed the Orloj's features. "Indeed. Tools remain powerless if you do not wield them. **Time** presses on. That clock I set for your final 24 hours does not slow. Every delay, every misstep, stokes the Goblin's illusions."

Thumbpee chimed in, tapping a tiny foot irritably. "And illusions *love* a lack of caution."

Greenie nodded, contrite. "We're trying—honestly. But the city is enormous, illusions at every turn. We never know if we're on the right path."

The Orloj leaned forward, swirling his teacup in large, calloused hands. "Rely on what you have learned—Generosity, Kindness, Clarity. The next mentor you seek will show you something new, yes, but you must not neglect the powers already in your grasp. Only by using them consistently can you fend off illusions before they ensnare you."

Caution from a Fatherly Clock

Finishing off a croissant, the Orloj fixed them with a gentle but firm stare. "The Goblin is cunning. He seizes on *any* hesitation—if you stall, argue, or doubt yourselves, illusions will descend. Use the lens at the first hint of trickery. Open your shield if illusions tug at your emotions. Each moment you waste may cost you dearly."

His words were not a new "virtue lesson," but a clear directive to tighten their approach. **Thumbpee** bobbed his head in emphatic agreement, while **Buggie** hovered above, shining flickers of green light that danced on the table.

Reddish exhaled slowly. "We understand. We can't keep repeating the same mistakes."

The Orloj's stern expression softened. "You have the strength and wisdom to prevail—if you truly *apply* them. I have watched you grow from young wizards in Prague, Venice, Paris… Now you stand on the brink of a power beyond Master Wizardry, but the path narrows. Keep your eyes open, your hearts steady."

Parting Words

With a satisfied nod, the Orloj stood, towering over them in his broad-chested human form. "Finish your breakfast, Harlequins. Then go—search out your next mentor. You have no more time to lose."

The Orloj gave **Buggie** a parting pat, and **Thumbpee** a quick wink. Then, in a swirl of faint golden motes, he **melted** seamlessly into the lively crowd of wizards, as though the city itself swallowed him up. One moment he was there—then he was gone.

The Harlequins had barely finished their enchanted pastries when **Buggie** chirped overhead, pointing down a street that abruptly opened into a gaping chasm. Broken cobblestones dangled in midair, flickering with telltale illusions.

Greenie peered over the edge, heart pounding. "Is it real or not?"

"Partly real," **Checkered** decided, testing the swirling emptiness with a summoned light. "We'll have to get across."

They remembered their **hovering** power from Venice—only one wizard at a time could float. Taking turns, they ferried each other across the illusory gap, weaving spells and passing supplies as illusions snapped below. Finally, they emerged on solid ground, hearts racing. **Reddish** quipped, "A spoonful of positivity might have helped, but apparently, so does a dash of levitation."

For a moment, they sat quietly, the empty chair a reminder of how fleeting such guidance could be. The calliope-like melody of a Merry-go-round could be felt in the distance.

They felt the **Orloj's** presence fade, its final counsel echoing in their minds:**"Where illusions loom darkest, keep wonder close."**

Thus, at the twilight end, they pressed onward—carrying the spark of Britain's **beloved** children's classics, ready to face illusions in the unfolding quest. Moments later, the creeping shadows parted, ushering them toward the **Tower of London** for the trials that would define illusions.

As the carousel's music faded, a faint scratch—like claws on distant stone—echoed briefly beyond the illusion's edge, unnoticed amid their laughter.

Mrs. V's Whirling Return

As the **Orloj**'s parting glow receded into the **lamp-lit** streets, the **Harlequins** lingered briefly, pondering its **fatherly** counsel on their earlier encounter—*use your virtues swiftly, illusions feed on hesitation*. Blunt glanced around the **moonlit** avenues of **Parallel London**, half expecting another illusion. Then, with a faint chirp, **Buggie** signaled a new direction.

They had barely taken two steps away from the Orloj's fading glow when a **kaleidoscope swirl of pastel colors** zigzagged across their path, showering them in glimmering motes. A familiar, gentle hum drifted on the magical breeze.

Greenie's eyes widened. "That energy—could it be—?"

Suddenly, the swirling motes converged, forming a diminutive, half-translucent figure: **Mrs. V.**, the kindly, long-deceased antiquarian from Hay-on-Wye. Her flowing cloak wavered between ethereal and real, and her eyes sparkled with ghostly warmth.

Mrs. V. (softly): "My dear young wizards. The Orloj has granted me a moment more—to share a final glimpse of wonder before your trials grow darker. Perhaps you wonder why I have returned to you, this time at the Orloj's behest. It is precisely because of its earlier counsel— 'keep wonder close.' And where else might wonder blossom more brightly, my dear wizards, than within the pages of England's most cherished tales? Thus, I shall guide you now to a street in Parallel London, woven intricately from the very fabric of Britain's timeless stories—each crafted to kindle the hearts and imaginations of those young enough, brave enough, to believe."

Mrs. V. waved a hand, conjuring a Peter Pan shadow that danced across the table—then morphed, a boy falling, eyes hollow. "Some lose their way chasing lost stars," she said, voice soft as a sigh. **Greenie** frowned, toast forgotten. "Is that our enemy?" Mrs. V.'s smile was cryptic, her gaze drifting to the Orloj. "Perhaps once," she murmured, "before shadows claimed him." The shadow dissolved, leaving a chill.

Blunt exhaled, a note of awe in his voice. "We thought…we'd never see you again."

Mrs. V.: "Time's tapestry is pliable in Parallel London, child. As I said earlier, I come bearing an invitation into the **Great British Storybook Tapestry**—a realm fashioned from Britain's most cherished children's tales."

She reached out with one shimmering hand, tracing a **door of rainbow-hued air**. Faint images of **flying umbrellas, pirate ships, and giant mushrooms** rippled across its surface.

Mrs. V. (with a reassuring nod): "Step through. Let these stories teach you how childlike wonder dispels illusions. For within these classic tales lies the purest magic—innocence, imagination, and hope—which illusions cannot corrupt.

Then, you must resume your Orloj quest—time is fleeting."

The Harlequins shared uncertain glances but felt the sincerity radiating from Mrs. V. Nodding, they followed her into the **iridescent portal**.

Entering the Patchwork Streets

They emerged onto a **single cobblestone lane** under a softly glowing sky. Each **segment** of the road was different: at one end stood quaint Edwardian row houses; halfway down, a lurid swirl of pirate sails loomed; beyond that, a whimsical candy-strewn walkway shimmered. A **chimney sweep**—cockney accent and all—stood tipping his sooty cap.

Chimney Sweep (broad grin): "Blimey! So, you've arrived. Welcome, guv'nors an' ladies, to **The Great British Storybook Tapestry**! Mind yer step—these illusions can be as slippery as rooftops in the rain."

He beckoned them forward, each Harlequin exchanging a giddy smile despite the urgency of their main quest.

Peter Pan: Starry Rooftop in "Neverland London"

At the lane's first bend, the houses **stretched upward**, merging into **a rooftop panorama** under swirling stars. A **green-clad boy** somersaulted overhead, **pixie dust** trailing behind him. He halted midair, eyeing the Harlequins with playful skepticism.

"Grown-ups always ruin the fun—are you sure you're ready to face illusions?"

Checkered stifled a laugh. "We do see illusions daily, but… can we truly fly past them?" Hands on hips, asks joyfully, Peter Pan.

"All it takes is **faith, trust, and a little bit of pixie dust!** If you believe you're stuck, illusions keep you grounded. Believe you can soar—well, up you go!"

To **prove it**, he darted to a narrow ravine bridging two rooftops. The gap below looked endless.

"Go on—try jumping. Happy thoughts, you lot!" instructs playfully, Peter Pan.

With a collective breath, the Harlequins leapt. For a heart-stopping moment, illusions tried to claw at their ankles, but the memory of **Peter Pan's** childlike confidence propelled them across safely. Landing with a whoop, they found themselves further along the lane, the star-studded sky morphing into dawn light. Peter's voice echoed behind:

"Never say goodbye—because goodbye means forgetting!" parts ways a fading Peter Pan.

Mary Poppins: A Chalk-Painted London Row

Next, the rooftops **melted into** a pastel-colored Edwardian Street. Soft **music** drifted on the breeze. A **cheerful nanny** descended from the sky, perched upon a **parrot-handled**

umbrella.

"Spit-spot, young wizards. This city's illusions are quite the mess. A spoonful of positivity, and perhaps you'll tidy them away?" while adjusting her hat, remarks sternly, Mary Poppins, **"Practically perfect in every way,"** seeking precision she added.

Reddish marveled, "You make it sound so easy…"

"In **every job that must be done**, there is an **element of fun**. Even illusions cannot withstand a dash of cheer, dear," rhymes an exuberant, Mary Poppins.

She pointed to a heavy crate sitting in the street, labeled "Doubts." Each Harlequin tried to lift it; illusions made it feel impossibly weighty. Mary Poppins winked and **sprinkled a spark of shimmering dust**. Encouraged, Firee grinned, focusing on a pleasant memory. Together, they lifted the crate easily.

"See? Light hearts lighten burdens. Now off with you—there's more to see." Remarks with a knowing now, Mary Poppins.

She **rose skyward** again, humming her melodic tune. The Harlequins marched on, renewed by her counsel.

Oliver Twist: A Grim Victorian Alley

The pastel street **darkened** abruptly into a **sooty Victorian alley**, gas lamps flickering. A small boy in ragged clothes approached, **battered bowl** in trembling hands.

"Please, sir… I—I want some more. W-would you help me carry this bread to others?" fearfully asks Oliver, is eyes pleading.

A swirl of illusions revealed ghostly children hunched at a workhouse door. Oliver looked ready to give up in despair. The Harlequins quickly **joined him**, distributing meager loaves to the spectral orphans. Illusions hissed—**why bother?** But Reddish shook her head, pressing on.

"Kindness can be scarce, but it's the one meal illusions can never steal… if you share it." Sheepishly says Oliver, his voice wavering.

Breezie knelt, smiling softly: "We won't forget."

Darkness lifted, the orphans flickered out with grateful smiles, and Oliver vanished around a corner. The lane brightened again.

Treasure Island: The Pirate Cove

A sudden gust of **salty wind** hit them. The street's paving stones **shifted** into a **pirate ship deck**. **Ropes** hung overhead; the cityscape replaced by rolling illusions of waves under a moonlit sky.

"X marks the spot, mates—but illusions mark the traps. **D'ye have the boldness to claim your fortune?"** Points Jim Hawkins clutching a treasure map.

Greenie stared at the swirling illusions of a **sea monster**. Jim motioned them to fend it off with confidence. The Harlequins brandished small spells, dissolving the monstrous shape in shimmering motes.

"Aye, only the bold find truth beneath illusions. Keep that compass of courage pointed straight. Now weigh anchor—your next port beckons!" Remarks a grinning Jim Hawkins

As quickly as it appeared, the pirate ship dissolved back into the lane.

Charlie and the Chocolate Factory: Candy-Stripes and Whimsy

Candy-striped illusions took hold, unveiling a whimsical **factory facade**, chocolate rivers swirling underfoot. A flamboyant man in a purple velvet coat—**Willy Wonka**—stood tipping his hat.

"Welcome to my empire of edible daydreams. In here you'll find Candy-striped illusions, chocolate rivers, candy trees—an entire walkway that "tastes like fruit" with each step. But watch your sweet tooth, dear wizards—**reality is so dull, best to color it in sweets**, though illusions might give you a cavity!" Welcomes the Harlequins, Wonka wearing a mischievous grin.

Checkered inhaled the chocolate-scented air, blinking. "This is… surreal."

"Marvelous, yes—and dangerous, too, **if your eyes outgrow your heart. Go on—taste imagination. But keep your wits about you!**" Handing each Harlequin a bright candy.

They popped the candies in their mouths. A surge of laughter and color washed over them, illusions swirling. "Don't forget what happened to the man who suddenly got everything he always wanted… He lived happily ever after," for a moment, cynicism melted away—a sense of **childlike nonsense** freed their minds.

"A little nonsense now and then is cherished by the wisest men. Now, onward—you've confections yet to discover in your quest," declares in joy a winking Wonka.

He vanished into a puff of sweet-scented smoke.

Alice's Adventures in Wonderland:
"Curiouser and Curiouser"

The candy-striped ground **shifted** to a **checkerboard path**. A **cheshire grin** flickered in the air, vanishing except for bright teeth. Everything around had distorted proportions, a corridor flashes with pastel colors; lined with signs pointing contradictory directions. Bizarre characters pop in and out of doors that seem to shrink or grow as they are opened or closed, a Cheshire Cat, a Mad Hatter, and a White Rabbit. Then a **young girl** in a blue dress stepped forward, eyeing them curiously.

"Oh my, you don't look half as puzzled as I was. Are you sure you're in the right dimension?" Aks bemused, Alice.

Greenie gave a tiny laugh. "We're never sure anymore."

"Perfect. **'Curiouser and curiouser,'** they say. I once learned that illusions—like riddles—unravel if you keep questioning. **Ask why the nonsense, and nonsense sometimes answers,**" states Alice with a mischievous smile.

A signpost behind Alice abruptly **swirled** with contradictory arrows, illusions swirling faster. The Harlequins tested each direction, discovering only one that wasn't blocked by illusions. They overcame the paradox.

"Look at that—you can navigate madness by staying curious. Farewell now—I've a tea party to attend," advises happily, a pleased Alice.

"We are all mad here… The sense that normal logic can fail in illusions—only curiosity and willingness to question can conquer them…Question everything; illusions rely on unexamined assumptions."

She gave a small curtsey and stepped behind a giant mushroom, **vanishing**.

The whimsical tales dissolved into a shimmer of gears, the Orloj's hum guiding them back to the Tower's shadowed depths, where a heavy door swung open to reveal a chamber of ancient war.

A Collective Reflection

At the lane's far end, the **Chimney Sweep** reappeared, tapping his sooty broom on the cobbles.

"Ye've had a taste o' the six finest children's tales in all Blighty. Any illusions your Goblin throws at ye—dismiss 'em with the wonder an' hope these stories taught ya."

He guided them to a final swirling portal, where **Mrs. V** waited, eyes bright with pride," narrates in heartwarming jumping verses, the jolly Chimney sweep.

"Peter Pan taught you belief over doubt, Mary Poppins the magic of positivity, Oliver Twist the power of compassion, Treasure Island the daring spirit to press on, Willy Wonka the playful nonsense that dethrones cynicism, and Alice the bravery to question illusions," narrates in loving grandmotherly voice, Mrs. V.

Blunt brushed away an emotional flutter. "Thank you. We'll remember these lessons… illusions can't stand against childlike wonder."

"You see, dear ones," she said softly, **"the Orloj's message of childlike wonder resonates in each story.** Whether it's magical flight, a spoonful of sugar, heartfelt compassion, or a daring quest, these classics remind you that illusions can't conquer a mind fueled by joy and belief."

Greenie blinked back tears. **"It'll be an unforgettable memory, Mrs. V."**

"Time to go, children. The Orloj's clock won't slow. Hold these stories in your heart," prompts Mrs., V. in a hurried voice.

Mrs. V. beckoned them toward a final **ripple in the air**—the gateway leading back to **Parallel London**.

"Hurry, the Goblin lurks. My time here wanes." Use what you've learned from these stories to stand strong against illusions."

Stepping Back into Parallel London

In a swirl of bright magic, the Harlequins **stepped through** the portal. One by one, the Harlequins ended their storybook journey, hearts warmed by the reminders of **Peter Pan**, **Mary Poppins**, **Willy Wonka**, **Alice**, **Oliver** and **Jim Hawkins**.

At once, the **cacophony of Parallel London** returned: floating lanterns, arcane wards, the distant hum of illusions. Mrs. V.'s presence faded, her final wave dissolving into glowing embers.

They found themselves **exactly where** they had been—**the vantage under Big Ben**, or near the swirling city corners— **only moments** after they left.

"Was those mere seconds in real time?" in awe stated Breezie.

Thumbpee huffed but flashed a begrudging smile. "Even illusions can't hamper your lesson in childlike wonder, I suppose."

Checkered and Firee exchanged determined glances.

Checkered: "We have these new insights. Let's put them to use—kindness, belief, curiosity… all the things that push illusions back."

Blunt nodded firmly. "We can't let the Goblin exploit our doubts. Let's keep going, no hesitation."

With renewed spirit—**and the memory of six timeless tales**—the Harlequins pressed deeper into Parallel London's enchanted streets, illusions lurking but their hearts fortified. **Peter Pan's** dare to fly, **Mary Poppins's** spoonful of positivity, **Oliver's** plea for kindness, **Jim Hawkins's** boldness, **Willy Wonka's** whimsical nonsense, and **Alice's** fearless curiosity all glowed within them like tiny lamps against the dark.

Moments later, as the creeping shadows parted, they felt the Orloj's silent beckoning once more—summoning them toward the Tower of London for the trials that would define their next illusions. But now, they carried the spark of Britain's beloved children's classics in their hearts, ready to combat whatever illusions dared to arise.

Chapter 7

Shadows of Sloth

Stepping cautiously through **Parallel London's** bustling mid-morning streets, the Harlequins felt excitement tempered by urgency. Their conversation with the Orloj had steeled their resolve—yet every lapse seemed to strengthen the **Dark Goblin** lingering in the city's magical shadows. Worse, they had no direct lead on their next mentor, and time ticked relentlessly onward.

"How do we even *begin* to find our next guide?" **Breezie** wondered, eyeing the winding lanes, each brimming with conjurers and wizard folk.

Blunt lifted **Clarity's Lens** but saw only faint, chaotic magical lines. "No obvious route," he admitted grimly.

Checkered stood firm. "We can't just wander. The Orloj emphasized using our powers and not succumbing to confusion. Let's stay focused."

Determined not to waste more hours, they ventured deeper into **Parallel London**. Illusions hung thick in the air, but they pressed forward. **Thumbpee** issued quick admonishments from Blunt's shoulder, while **Buggie** glided above, scanning for wards and traps.

A Luring Melody

Suddenly, **Buggie** darted down, chirping urgently. Above, a **haunting melody** drifted across rooftops. **Firee** recognized it immediately. "The Pied Piper—he's calling us again!"

Roused by fresh purpose, they invoked **Sticky Fingers**, scaling an old building's facade. Their hearts pounded at the dizzying vantage: **Parallel London** sprawled in a mosaic of slanted rooftops, chimneys under a pale magical sky. Far ahead, the **Pied Piper** skipped from roof to roof, beckoning with his flute's eerie tune.

But each step overhead was **dangerous**: crumbling tiles, wards sparking illusions, shadows lunging from hidden corners. Still, they pushed onward, refusing to be deterred by fatigue.

Dark Goblin's Snare

Midway across precarious rooftops near **Tower Bridge**, **darkness** surged, forming shadowy tendrils that snatched them off their feet. An ominous laugh echoed: the **Dark Goblin**.

"So determined…yet that urge to *quit* tugs at you," the Goblin sneered. "**Sloth** offers relief when the climb is too steep. Surrender to laziness, and I might spare you."

Suspended above the **churning Thames**, panic flared. **Blunt** tried to summon Clarity's Lens, but fear blurred his focus.

Breezie cried, "Together! **Empath's Sight**—don't let illusions make us give up!"

A **warm pulse** united them, dispelling illusions that whispered *just rest—stop trying*. Realizing the Goblin thrived on *slothful surrender*, **Checkered** shouted,

"Sloth has no power here! We keep going, no matter how hard!"

Their collective resolve eroded the tendrils. They crashed onto various rooftops, battered yet free. In the chaos, **Firee** and **Greenie** lost footing, plunging into the river below.

Rescue from the River

Lightning reflexes kicked in. **Checkered** invoked **"Heart's Shield!"** to repel despair illusions. Meanwhile, **Breezie** dove into the Thames after Firee and Greenie. Moments later, he surfaced, pulling them ashore. Drenched but relieved, both wore determined expressions.

"We almost…just quit," **Greenie** admitted, shivering. "But we *didn't*," **Firee** said, breath unsteady. "We overcame it."

The Piper's Final Note

Once more, the **Pied Piper's** tune rose, leading them across battered ledges until the melody vanished by a **modest, ivy-draped door** perched among ancient chimneys. The note of the flute ended abruptly, leaving an etched sign:

"Dillibrante and Dillettante Antiquarians"

(Est. a century and half ago)

Inside, **Lettizia Dillettante** stood calmly—tall, hair threaded with white, her ankle-length skirt whispering across the bookstore's wooden floor, her gaze both compassionate and firm. Moonlight from a high window illuminated her pale skin, accentuating the aquiline curve of her nose and the subtle flicker in her milky blue eyes. Long, white-threaded hair draped over her shoulders, lending her a statuesque grace. Despite her refined bearing, a steely determination coursed through her every gesture. "Perseverance," she pronounced, her cool voice unwavering, "is forged like iron. **The fire of difficulties only tempers it.**"

"You flirted with **Sloth** today," she said softly, voice resonant. "One step more, and you might never have found me."

Lettizia's words wove a tapestry of grit, each thread a challenge to outlast the fraying edge of despair.

She guided them into a **mazelike bookstore**, the shelves lit by drifting orbs. "Sloth robs you of the will to press on—only **Perseverance** conquers it."

Three Poems: Discipline, Impetus, Perseverance

Leading them to a **glowing table** in the center, Lettizia addressed them earnestly. "But perseverance doesn't stand alone. It is built upon **Discipline** and **Impetus**—two vital forces. Permit me to share three poems."

She opened a heavy tome, flipping to a first section:

*

"Discipline"

Discipline is a virtue we aren't born with.

Hence, it's a code of conduct we must cultivate,

an imperative condition

to consistently achieve any goal,

a prerequisite of success,

and work extremely hard for

as we build/growth it into an unassailable HABIT.

When (or until) discipline becomes a deeply ingrained HABIT,

it'll feel heavy,

and a drag that we easily and perennially find

excuses to avoid.

To the contrary when it becomes a

"kind of" military routine

then it becomes an almost unnoticeable virtue,

in the pursuit of endless achievements,

and above all "Excellence"

on anything we embark on in life.

*

Lettizia glanced up. "Without discipline, you'll crumble under illusions that tempt you to drift. **What does discipline mean to you?"**

Blunt answered thoughtfully, "It's the steady commitment to act, even when it's inconvenient. It transforms fleeting effort into reliable habit."

Lettizia nodded. "Precisely. Now, the second poem."

*

"Impetus"

When desire shines and sparkles,

and yet,

is impregnated with ingenuity and enthusiasm.

When intense energy bursts in spades,

When ebullient predisposition erupts unstoppable,

When our drive is impregnated with "tunnel-vision,"

When we are obsessively "bulls-eye centric,"

while taking action,

embarking on anything in life,

Impetus is an existentially vital virtue,

a force to be reckoned with,

as it provides us with indestructible foundations,

supporting an endless inner strength,

an unwavering, relentless desire,

and an unbreakable, steely determination,

to toil and toil and toil,

until we prevail and conquer,

by reaching our wildest,

our most impossible, improbable dreams,

those extraordinary oneiric journeys

where impetus is an essential ingredient,

a required component,

to reach those life-crests,

seemingly unattainable pinnacles,

that only the "impetuous" ride

in the topsy-turvy, merry-go-round

of our precious, but very brief existence.

*

She looked expectantly at them. "What do you glean from impetus?"

Checkered ventured, "It's the fire that fuels discipline, the raw drive that pushes us forward—like a rushing current of motivation."

"Excellent," Lettizia said, satisfied. "And now, for the keystone poem."

*

"Perseverance"

The Engine and Fuel of Perseverance

At the heart of all great feats,
Where effort and ambition meet,
There lies a force, unwavering, bright—
Discipline, the guiding light.

Not fleeting fire, nor fickle will,
But steadiness, composed and still.
It builds the bridge, it clears the way,
Where lesser souls are led astray.

Yet even steel must bend to forge,
And engines fail without their source.
What moves the feet, what keeps them true?
What fuels the soul to push on through?

The impetus that drives this force,

That stirs the will and charts the course,
Is zeal, is grit, is burning fire,
An ember fed by fierce desire.

Through storms that rage and trials steep,
Indomitable hearts refuse to sleep.
With relentless drive and steadiness true,
They carve the path that few pursue.

With grit unshaken, minds refined,
Through trials fierce, through tasks designed,
It tempers fire, sharpens steel,
Transforms resolve to something real.

Relentless hands carve fate anew,
Through stubborn, immutable view.
For those who stand with focused might,
No mountain veils the summit's light.

Not fleeting fire nor fleeting might,
But stubborn, immutable in the fight.
With iron-willed, unassailable grace,
They rise again, they hold their place.

Each step they take, with measured pace,

An unassailable embrace,
Of hardship, toil, and unseen scars,
That forge the souls that reach the stars.

Through zeal and effort, inch by inch,
They hold the line; they will not flinch.
For resilience fuels their relentless climb,
Through endless walls, through endless time.

Yet effort alone cannot sustain,
Without a purpose, clear and plain.
What moves the hands, what sparks the mind,
What fuels the fire time after time?

It is belief, it is resolve,
A vision firm, a fate evolved.
A purpose set, a calling clear,
That makes them rise year after year.

Determination lights the way,
Through herculean tasks, they stay.
For perseverance is the mark
Of those who conquer in the dark.

And thus, they rise, again, again,

Until the world must now contend,

That those who walk this path of gold,

Will claim the dreams they dared behold.

For perseverance, forged in fire,

Builds virtuous circles, climbing higher.

To finish tasks, to reach, to soar,

To break past limits, and be no more—

A dreamer lost in idle schemes,

But one who makes—not one who dreams.

*

Lettizia closed the tome softly. "Perseverance is the virtue that directly defeats sloth. **Discipline** keeps you consistent, and **impetus** energizes your drive. Combine them, and you push on, no matter how illusions coax you to quit."

A Thorough Test

With a wave of her hand, the store's aisles elongated, forming a **magical gauntlet**. Weighted illusions pressed down on the Harlequins, each step feeling like wading through thick mud. Cozy chairs emerged, illusions urging them to *stop, relax*. But recalling Lettizia's words, they **pushed forward**—discipline overriding fatigue, impetus lighting their minds with unstoppable drive, perseverance fueling each footstep. In time, they reached the far end of the store, illusions scattered behind.

Checkered's legs burned as Pretoria's dust clouded her sight—an old race, her father's face in the crowd, disappointed.

"You quit," he mouthed, turning away.

She'd stopped mid-stride, lungs failing her.

Now, Lettizia's task loomed, endless. "I can't," **Checkered** wheezed, humor fading. "Perseverance outlasts despair," Lettizia urged.

Checkered grit her teeth, seeing that finish line again. "Not this time," she growled.

Lettizia nodded approvingly. "You see how these three unite to defeat sloth. *Never* lose them."

Sigil of Endurance

She presented **Blunt** a folded parchment. "You've earned the **Sigil of Endurance**—the synergy of discipline, impetus, and perseverance. Use it well; sloth often reappears in subtler forms."

Reddish carefully opened it. A faint golden symbol shimmered, resonating with the Harlequins' combined energies. Each felt a deeper sense of wholeness, an anchored resolve in their bones.

A fleeting shadow darted across the armory's far wall, gone before Reddish could turn, as if something tracked their faltering steps.

"Stand tall against illusions of laziness," Lettizia said gently. "Even small acts of forward motion break sloth's hold."

A Final Caution

Her usually intense gaze softened. "I came close to ruin once, paralyzed by the thought that trying further was pointless. A dear friend's unwavering push awakened my impetus—then discipline, and at last perseverance. Embrace all three, or illusions will devour your will."

She glanced at each Harlequin in turn, her fine features revealing measured pride. "I've walked these corridors of despair myself," she admitted. "But grit and discipline saw me through. Never doubt that you can endure, no matter how illusions press you."

In a swirl of soft light, **Lettizia** faded into the shelves. The store itself flickered, dissolving until the Harlequins found themselves once more on a **lonely rooftop** under Parallel London's now-bright sky.

Thumbpee gave a grudgingly respectful nod. "At least you overcame sloth *and* learned the triad behind perseverance. But time is running short—move!"

Renewed Resolve

Clutching the Sigil of Endurance, the Harlequins felt a fresh synergy: **discipline** to be consistent, **impetus** to energize them, **perseverance** to carry them through. Below, the **Dark Goblin** undoubtedly fumed, but they no longer feared giving up. Each step forward carried them closer to the Orloj's final secret.

In the distance, illusions danced across **Parallel London**'s skyline. The Goblin lurked somewhere beyond, preparing the next trial. Yet the Harlequins descended from the rooftop with unshakable fortitude. If the path was arduous, so be it—they would face it with discipline, impetus, and perseverance united as one.

Dark Goblin (voice echoing): "You never cared when I fell. Unity was for the chosen… not for the broken."

The corridor went silent. Breezie shivered.

Revelations of the Goblin's Past

Breezie: **"He wasn't just some monster. He was one of our mentors… once."**

Blunt (softly): "We must end this. And maybe…somehow… help him?"

Their resolve firmed under the flickering lamplight; the path ahead uncertain but unyielding.

Chapter 8

Shadows of Arrogance

An uneasy silence fell as they crossed the deserted courtyard, the Tower's spires looming. **Reddish** paused, scanning the gloom. "I've got that feeling again…like we're about to be hit."

Their **danger sense**—gifted in Paris—throbbed alarmingly. At the same moment, a hooded figure shuffled out, feigning friendliness. **Blunt** narrowed his eyes, focusing on **mind-reading**. A swirl of malicious intent rippled behind the figure's calm smile.

"He's baiting us," **Blunt** murmured, urging the group back. **Firee** readied a defensive stance. The illusions started unraveling around the hooded figure, but forewarned by **danger sense**, the Harlequins swiftly retreated. "We'll face the next illusions on our terms, not his," **Checkered** said resolutely, forging ahead.

A **sullen twilight** cloaked Parallel London, painting the streets in dusky purples and fading gold. The Harlequins trudged forward; hearts uneasy after their grueling trials with Sloth. Though they had prevailed, a new tension now simmered among them—small but palpable. **Thumbpee**, perched on Blunt's shoulder, had sensed it first: a creeping, subtle **pride** that made them overconfident in small decisions, dismissive of each other's input.

"Careful," **Thumbpee** cautioned, voice stern. "Arrogance is the easiest trap for strong wizards. The Goblin loves inflated egos."

Yet the group pressed on, their footsteps echoing across **cobbled avenues** lined with curious shops. Flickers of illusions teased at corners: swirling ribbons of color or ephemeral laughter that vanished when approached. **Buggie** soared overhead, shining bright green beams at possible leads, but each alley ended in illusions that teased them with false entrances or dissolving doorways.

A Subtle Rift

Pausing by a fountain in a quiet square, **Firee** exhaled with frustration. "We're better wizards than this. Why can't we see through illusions quicker?"

Reddish shrugged, crossing her arms. "Maybe we're overthinking. We *are* Master Wizards now—shouldn't illusions be child's play?"

Greenie shot them a concerned look. "We *are* strong, but the illusions keep twisting the city's reality. Let's not underestimate them."

Checkered nodded quietly. "Agreed. Overconfidence might sabotage us."

Blunt set his jaw. "We'll find the next mentor soon. We're good enough to handle anything."

In that moment, an almost **invisible** tension passed between them—small flickers of pride that whispered *we're strong, illusions can't fool us.*

Thumbpee frowned, muttering under his breath. "Arrogance has snared bigger fish. Beware."

A Dead-End…or So It Seemed

They followed **Buggie**'s glow to an old street overshadowed by a tall Victorian facade. The door at the end looked enticingly like an antiquarian's shop, letters half-faded. Rushing closer, they realized it was a **dead-end** courtyard. A mocking laugh echoed overhead.

"Running in circles?" the **Dark Goblin** sneered from a ledge. "Is your grand wizardry not enough to see the correct path?"

The group bristled, stung by the insult. The Goblin vanished with a swirl of shadows. Silence draped the alley, tension thickening.

Reddish snapped, "We can handle him if he'd just face us properly."

Checkered pressed a calming hand on Reddish's shoulder. "Don't let him taunt us into rash moves."

The Illusion of Grandeur

Without warning, illusions flared: the battered alley melted into a vision of triumph—a grand palace courtyard celebrating the Harlequins as heroes. Applauding crowds, banners proclaiming them the "Greatest Wizards." The sudden adoration felt euphoric.

Greenie blinked, enthralled by the cheers. "This…feels so good. Finally recognized for our power!"

Firee almost smiled along—then reeled back. "Wait—this is too easy. It's a trap."

But the illusions pressed in, voices praising each wizard: "Oh, masterful Checkered, you are unbeatable! Reddish, unstoppable force!" The applause threatened to submerge them in **self-satisfaction**.

Blunt tried to activate Clarity's Lens, but the wave of adulation made him hesitate.

Why destroy a scene that glorifies us?

He caught himself, heart pounding. "No… we must see truth. Don't let arrogance blind us!"

Forcing the lens to clarity, illusions cracked and fell away, revealing the plain alley once more. A disappointed hiss echoed: the **Dark Goblin** had nearly snared them with false grandeur.

An Unexpected Shop:

A subtle shimmer rippled across a side wall. Letters formed:

"Van Egmond Antiquarians"
(Est. who knows how long ago)

The door appeared where a blank brick surface had been. Slipping inside, they found themselves in a **cozy, high-ceilinged bookstore** lined with ancient tomes, softly lit by drifting magical lanterns. Shelves parted, revealing **Lucrecia Van Egmond**. She stood head and shoulders above most, a Nordic figure with a calm, self-aware poise. Her blond hair was swept into a practical ponytail, accentuating the elegant lines of her neck. Her clothing was simple yet regal, hinting at a Mediterranean flair despite her Scandinavian appearance.

"Humility," she said quietly, voice carrying a faint accent neither purely Northern nor Southern. "It is the power that mends a rift. Pride may keep you from apologizing, but illusions thrive on Arrogance. Letting it go frees you to see the truth."

She pressed her palms together in a humble gesture. "I learned humility the hard way," she confessed softly. "Don't let illusions turn your heart cold. Even the darkest arrogance can be undone with time…and a willingness to see beyond pride and ego."

Mrs. Van Egmond opened a large, leather-bound volume:

*

"The Fall of Lord Avenhurst"

Lord Avenhurst stood atop his grand balcony, gazing over his vast kingdom with satisfaction. His castle, towering over the valley, was a monument to his success—his conquests, his wealth, his unchallenged rule. To him, power was everything, and humility was for the weak.

One day, an old scholar named Elias requested an audience. The man, frail and weathered, was known for his wisdom. Amused, Lord Avenhurst granted him entrance.

"My Lord," Elias said, bowing deeply, "I bring you a warning. The foundation of a kingdom is not stone nor gold, but the loyalty of its people. Treat them with kindness, lest your walls crumble from within."

Lord Avenhurst scoffed. "Loyalty is bought with power, not kindness. My people serve because they fear me. That is enough."

Elias sighed. "A tree stands tall, believing itself indestructible, but it is the unseen rot within that fells it."

The lord dismissed him with a wave.

Seasons passed, and Lord Avenhurst's pride swelled further. He taxed his people heavily, built monuments to himself, and crushed dissent with an iron fist. The more he took, the more he demanded, certain that his power was eternal.

But one winter night, when the castle's golden halls should have glowed with warmth, torches flickered in the distant hills. The people, weary of his rule, had gathered in rebellion. His soldiers, once loyal, abandoned their posts. The walls of his castle, once impenetrable, were thrown open from within.

Lord Avenhurst fled to the highest tower, watching in disbelief as his mighty fortress fell—not to an enemy army, but to the people he had scorned.

As flames licked the sky, he remembered Elias's words. A kingdom is not stone nor gold, but the hearts of those who serve it. And hearts, once turned, will not return.

By dawn, his rule was dust, his pride his downfall.

*

When **Lucrecia** concluded, she gazed at the Harlequins gravely. "**Arrogance** blinds one to reality. Lord Avenhurst believed he was invincible. In ignoring others, he planted the seeds of his downfall. In our age, too, lords of steel and circuits crumble when pride blinds them," Lucrecia mused."

Checkered frowned, reflecting. "He lost everything not to an outside enemy, but his own pride."

Lucrecia nodded, her milky blue eyes reflecting empathy. "The greatest fortress is worthless if *within* rots. Pride robs you of allies, shutting your ears to warnings."

Next, she turned to a slimmer, gilded booklet:

*

"Arrogance"

Arrogance is pride, twisted cruel,
A reckless fire, fierce but fueled
By hollow echoes, self-deceit,
A gilded mask with hollow feet.

It struts upon the fragile thread,
A tower built on words unsaid,
Blind to warnings, deaf to grace,
A mirror's love, a lone embrace.

Pride whispers lies— You stand alone!
Yet isolation chills the bone.
It crowns itself in hollow might,
But dims the stars, obscures the light.

With careless scorn, it casts aside
The steady hands that once allied,
Till wisdom flees, till echoes fade,
Till all that's left is loss, betrayed.

Yet where pride crumbles, humbled eyes
Unveil the truth, embrace the wise—

For strength is not the lone command,

But hearts united, hand in hand.

No storm can break the bonds we weave,

No night can steal what we believe.

True power dwells where souls unite,

Where love stands firm, where hearts burn bright.

*

Closing the poem, **Lucrecia** asked gently, "So, what have you learned from these lines?"

Breezie spoke first, voice hushed. "Arrogance is isolation. It says, 'I need no one else.' But real power is built with others—humility fosters unity."

Reddish added, "Pride lies to us, claiming we're beyond mistakes. But ignoring mistakes leads to downfall."

Lucrecia's eyes glimmered approval. "Precisely. **Humility** stands as the antidote to arrogance. It opens your ears, your hearts. It prevents illusions from exploiting your overconfidence."

An Illusory Trial

A swirl of **magical** motion transformed the store's center into a **grand hall** with mirrored walls. Each Harlequin glimpsed an idealized reflection: themselves in regal robes, commanding throngs. The reflections whispered seductive flattery, urging them to belittle others.

But recalling the short story and poem, they recognized the trap. **Greenie** turned away from her reflection. **Firee** refused the praising illusions, invoking humility. One by one, they stepped out of the mirrored illusions, rejecting vain flattery. The illusions shattered, leaving the store quiet once more.

A faint hiss, barely audible over the mirrors' vibrations, slithered through the corridor, as if a hidden watcher reveled in the clones' taunts.

A New Power: The Mirror of Humility

Lucrecia Van Egmond smiled, retrieving a **hand-sized mirror** from a drawer. "You've faced illusions feeding arrogance and proven your humility. Take this: **the Mirror of Humility**. When activated, it reflects the *truth* behind prideful illusions—your own or others'—shattering them with honest insight."

She extended it to **Blunt**, who accepted it, feeling a soft glow of recognition. The polished surface shimmered with subtle runes.

"Arrogance thrives in darkness," **Lucrecia** said quietly, "while humility is light.

Keep that light bright, or illusions will devour you from within."

Parting Words

Lucrecia Van Egmond's form began to fade amid drifting motes of color. "Remember Lord Avenhurst's downfall. Pride forms cracks in your foundation, unseen until too late. With humility, you stand open to wisdom—and to each other."

Stepping through the creaking door, they emerged into Parallel London's night, the air thrumming as Big Ben's distant face pulsed with the Orloj's ancient voice.

Before they could thank her, the entire bookstore dissolved, leaving them in the now-deserted alleyway. The faint hum of Parallel London's distant bustle returned, as though the shop never existed.

Thumbpee perched crossly on Blunt's shoulder, arms folded. "Arrogance overcame. Good. Don't let illusions of grandeur snare you again, or the Goblin will feast."

Renewed and Humbled

Clutching the **Mirror of Humility**, the Harlequins exchanged sober looks. They'd tasted illusions that flattered them with false greatness—and realized how dangerously tempting that was. Yet they overcame it by remembering their bond and acknowledging they weren't invincible alone.

Somewhere in the shadows, the **Dark Goblin** undoubtedly seethed, robbed yet again of a victory. But they no longer feared illusions of inflated pride. With **humility** guiding them, they walked on, alert for the next test—and the final unveiling of London's elusive Orloj.

Chapter 9

Twilight's Summons:

The Orloj's Second Counsel

Early evening draped Parallel London in shades of amber and violet, the city's noise settling to a low hum, as though it anticipated something momentous. Under the **looming silhouette** of Big Ben, the Harlequins paused, hearts thrumming with equal parts excitement and trepidation. The clock face glowed faintly above, a steady pulse tugging them forward.

At the base of **Big Ben**, the cobblestones vibrated with a low, gentle **hum** that resonated through their bones. Suddenly, the **Orloj** appeared in his powerful human form, stepping out from shifting lamplight as though he'd always been there—broad, burly shoulders, a fatherly glint in his deep-set eyes.

"Welcome back, Harlequins." His voice wrapped around them in a comforting yet commanding warmth.

Blunt stepped forward, managing a respectful bow. "We return stronger… but also humbled."

Reddish nodded quietly. "We've faced illusions of arrogance and despair; we learned humility, perseverance."

A small smile softened the Orloj's otherwise stern features. "You have done well," he affirmed, voice resonating with approval. "But you tread a narrowing – narrow path. Tell me— what do you now understand of **arrogance**?"

Checkered caught the hint of caution in the Orloj's tone. "Arrogance is a trap," she answered. "Pride blinds us to our flaws. *Humility* keeps us honest and united."

The Orloj inclined his head. "And **despair**?"

Breezie exhaled. "It's a crippling darkness feeding off lost hope. **Perseverance** broke its hold, reminding us to rise no matter how deep we'd sunk."

The Orloj's gaze flickered with satisfaction. Yet, beneath the warmth, a warning lingered. "You have grown indeed—**Mirror of Humility** and **Dust of Resolve** were rightly earned. But remember," he said, voice dropping in gravity, "tools remain useless if you do not wield them **quickly and consistently**. Arrogance or despair may ambush you the moment you falter."

Firee swallowed, tension evident. "The Dark Goblin… can you sense how close he is now?"

A somber light shadowed the Orloj's expression. "Closer than ever. Eager to exploit any lapse—be it overconfidence, hesitation, or distrust among you."

A Fatherly Reminder

He folded his arms across his broad chest, posture radiating calm authority. "Each time illusions ensnared you; you hesitated before using your powers. *Do not* repeat that mistake. If your lens or mirror remain idle until the trap is closing, the Goblin gains ground."

Thumbpee hopped from Blunt's shoulder with a brusque nod. "Exactly. *Half your trouble stems from waiting too long.*"

Greenie lowered her gaze, recalling close calls. "We do try… but illusions come so fast, and we're tired."

The Orloj's voice gentled, though it remained firm. "Tired, yes, but you have the **Dust of Resolve**. You overcame despair. *Trust your unity.* Use your mirror the instant pride or confusion creeps in. Work as one, or illusions will tear you apart."

No New Virtue—Yet a Critical Warning

Sensing the Harlequins' mixture of relief and tension, the Orloj softened his stance. "I bestow no new lesson here, only a charge to better apply what you've learned. The final confrontation draws near, and the Goblin is cunning. *Remember your humility, your perseverance.* If either lapse, illusions will devour your confidence—and your bond."

They nodded gravely, absorbing the paternal advice. **Reddish** met the Orloj's eyes, voice quiet yet resolute. "We understand. We won't let arrogance or despair slip back in unchallenged."

The Orloj gave a satisfied, fatherly grunt. "Good. Then hold fast to clarity. Think quickly, act decisively. Your greatest danger now is *complacency*—believing you're beyond further illusions because you've succeeded once."

A Subtle Foreshadowing

From somewhere behind the Orloj, **Buggie** buzzed in tight circles, shining a cautious beam of green light up the tower's worn stones. **Thumbpee** hopped impatiently. The Orloj glanced at them, then turned back to the Harlequins.

"**He** grows bold," the Orloj rumbled quietly, a note of concern in his voice. "Watch the shadows. The Goblin hunts for cracks in your unity. If you stand unwavering, he cannot break you. If you falter… all you've gained may be forfeit."

Checkered shivered despite herself. "We'll stay vigilant."

Departure into the Twilight

A final swirl of **golden motes** drifted around the Orloj, faint light reflecting off Big Ben's clock face. **Evening** deepened, shadows stretching. The Orloj stepped back, beginning to dissolve into the city's magic, yet his voice lingered, resonating on the soft breeze:

"The final challenges approach, dear Harlequins. Be brave, and let your virtues guide you."

Then, as if breathing the lamplight in reverse, he vanished into the twilight, leaving them standing near Big Ben's monumental stones. The faint hum subsided, though the sense of watchful presence remained.

For a few moments, no one spoke—each grappling with the Orloj's fatherly *yet stern* counsel. They had come far, but the path narrowed, illusions thickened, and the Goblin prowled.

Blunt exhaled, gazing up at the softly glowing clock face. "Let's not forget his warning. We can't be slow or hesitant next time."

Reddish nodded firmly; Mirror of Humility clutched in one hand. "Nor let pride slip back in. We're still vulnerable."

Checkered offered a tentative smile. "At least we're together—and that might be our strongest shield."

Breezie answered quietly, but with conviction. "Yes… together."

And so, renewed by the Orloj's second visitation, the Harlequins turned once more into the twisting streets of **Parallel London**, hearts braced against illusions, minds keenly aware of how close the Goblin lurked. Though no brand-new virtue was taught, they recognized the deeper truth: sometimes the greatest challenge is staying true to what they already know—using humility and perseverance swiftly, effectively, and in unison.

An encounter with the Master

As the Orloj vanished into the lamp-lit crowd, the Harlequins stood **uncertain**. No new virtue had been named, and they weren't sure where illusions might strike next. Surveying the **moonlit alleys**, they resolved to stay alert for any anomaly. Just then, **Buggie** let out a sharp chirp—his tiny green beam pointing insistently across the Thames toward the **Globe Theatre**.

The Globe's Whisper

They'd barely caught their breath after the last ordeal when **Buggie** let out a shrill chirp, zipping around Blunt's head. His tiny green laser flickered insistently in the direction of the South Bank—toward the reconstructed **Globe Theatre** that loomed against the **moonlit sky**.

"What is it?" Checkered asked, brow furrowing as she peered at the half-timbered structure.

"Some echo of old London?" suggested Firee, stepping warily over mossy cobblestones.

All around them, **Parallel London** shimmered with leftover illusions, but the path to the Globe stood oddly clear—like a stage awaiting actors.

Suddenly, **Cornelius Tetragor** materialized at the edge of the street, robes trailing, long white beard swaying in the breeze. He offered them a knowing smile.

"Young wizards," he said in a calm yet urgent tone. **"Time's tapestry** frays here. The **Orloj** calls us to a place of words and wit. Follow me."

Thumbpee crossed his arms on Blunt's shoulder. "No more dithering," he muttered. "We've wasted enough hours."

The Harlequins exchanged determined glances and fell in step behind **Tetragor**. In hushed excitement, they approached the Globe's outer walls. The faint smell of tallow candles and freshly sawed oak drifted on the night air. A sign reading "Globe Theatre" swayed gently overhead.

"Look," Greenie whispered, pointing at a flicker of blurry air forming in the backstage shadows. "Another portal?"

Tetragor nodded gravely. "Yes—and one we must enter before illusions mislead us again. **Shakespeare's** realm awaits."

He gestured with two fingers, drawing a glowing astral line in midair. The thin, shimmering boundary widened into a portal of swirling grays and silvers. A surge of **Elizabethan** pipes and lutes whispered from the other side, mingling with the crackle of a fire.

"Stay close," **Tetragor** murmured, stepping through the swirling threshold first.

The Harlequins cast one last glance at modern London's looming skyscrapers across the Thames, hearts pounding. Then, in a single breath, they followed their mentor into the haze.

"We're truly stepping back four centuries," Reddish murmured, adrenaline brightening her eyes.

"Yes," Blunt confirmed, voice steady. "And if **Tetragor** says the **Orloj** calls us here, it must be vital."

A fleeting pilgrimage to the Globe, where Shakespeare's echoes draped the air in velvet tragedy.

Across the Portal

Instantly, the roar of distant traffic faded to be replaced by the clip-clop of horse hooves on cobblestones. Instead of electric lampposts, iron sconces cast flickering orange pools of light along a mud-caked road. A heavy, inky twilight pressed down.

Before them rose a circular playhouse, half thatched, half timbered, bustling with **Elizabethan Londoners**. Laughter and shouts of tradesmen drifted across a wooden bridge. **Tetragor** beckoned them forward with a solemn hush.

"Remember," he whispered, "they cannot see or hear us. We are watchers. Let the **Orloj** open your eyes to the seeds of creativity that shaped centuries."

An actor called out lines from the stage, though muffled by a door. The Harlequins, enthralled, felt they were eavesdropping on a timeless secret.

"We're truly inside his world," Checkered marveled, stepping gingerly to avoid tangling her foot in a coiled rope.

"Precisely," **Tetragor** said with quiet pride. "**William Shakespeare's** genius was once just daring words on crude parchment—yet it endures."

A swirl of stage-lantern smoke drifted past. With every breath, they sensed the magic of mortal artistry merging with the **Orloj's** hidden design. The Harlequins had glimpsed France's masters—now they stood poised to encounter an English legend on his home ground, all thanks to a single nudge from illusions at the Globe's door.

And so, in a swirl of theatrical illusions, they followed **Cornelius Tetragor** into **Elizabethan London**, oblivious that their next steps would bring them face to face with **the Bard** himself…

A Stroll with Shakespeare

"Young wizards, step lively," says **Cornelius Tetragor**, adjusting his long white robe as he marches through a swirling portal of blurry air. "I've brought you to the late sixteenth century—a London brimming with theatrical genius."

They emerge onto a cobbled street lined with timbered houses. A faint tang of wood smoke and roasting meats drifts by. Up ahead stands a half-timbered playhouse—the **Globe**— its thatched roof and open-air balcony abuzz with townsfolk in rough woolen cloaks and hats.

"We're actually here?" Reddish breathes, eyes wide at the **Elizabethan** bustle.

Tetragor lifts a finger, urging silence. "This realm cannot see or hear us. Observe, but do not interfere." He steps quietly inside the Globe, ushering them behind wooden benches. Torches and flickering lanterns cast dancing shadows over the stage.

Onstage, they spot a slim figure wearing a simple doublet and sporting a trim beard. Ink-stained quill in hand, he paces, muttering lines under his breath. An actor stands nearby, reading from a script:

"But soft! what light through yonder window breaks?"

Checkered whispers, "That's…**'Romeo and Juliet.'** Are we truly watching **William Shakespeare** at work?"

Cornelius Tetragor smiles. "Precisely. He's revising lines even as the actors rehearse. The plays as we know them never sprang fully formed—**Shakespeare** constantly tweaked them on his feet."

The Harlequins stand transfixed. They glimpse a swirl of scribbled pages, ephemeral illusions forming in midair. Monologues fade in and out of existence as if shaped by raw creativity. **Shakespeare** confers with an actor, pantomimes a dramatic gesture, then furiously crosses out lines on parchment.

"He was once unknown—just an ambitious writer," **Tetragor** says softly. "Yet his words revolutionized theater and the

English language. The city's illusions might fade, but these lines endure centuries."

Suddenly, a loud flourish of trumpets signals the start of a scene. The watchers freeze at their vantage. **Shakespeare** mumbles, nods, waves the actor to proceed—and the entire stage seems to glow with the promise of timeless stories.

They lingered a moment longer in **Shakespeare's** realm, hearts brimming with fascination. But as a drumroll signaled the start of another scene, **Cornelius Tetragor** raised his hand in silent command. A gentle glow pulsed around them—**the portal's** soft shimmer reactivating in the nearby shadows.

"Come," **Tetragor** murmurs, guiding them back to the side door.

Shakespeare was gesturing animatedly with his quill, too immersed in his craft to sense the hidden onlookers.

"We must return. You've had a glimpse of the Bard's workshop—carry forward the understanding that imagination and resilience can transform even the humblest stage into a realm of wonder."

Reluctantly, the **Harlequins** stepped toward the swirling boundary of blurry air. One by one, they slipped through, feeling the heady rush of centuries collapsing around them. The clip-clop of horse hooves faded into a distant hum, replaced by the modern hush of **Parallel London's** enchanted streets.

They emerged back at the **spot** from which they'd first followed **Buggie** toward the Globe—still illuminated by ghostly lanterns and reflecting the **Orloj's** fading luminance in the distance. **Thumbpee** clicked his tongue in mild impatience, but a hint of admiration shone in his eyes.

As they stepped from the Globe's wooden shadows, a single claw mark marred a nearby beam, its fresh gouge glinting in the twilight—unseen by the bustling crowd.

"We've glimpsed the Bard," Blunt murmured reverently, exchanging a look of excitement with Checkered. **"That was…incredible."**

Tetragor offered them a knowing smile. **"Hold this memory close, young wizards. His words outlived ages of illusions; so, shall your resolve outlast these trials."**

He nodded a silent farewell, then dissolved into the **lamp-lit** crowd just as the **Orloj** had done earlier. The Harlequins were left standing in the soft gloom, hearts brimming with fresh wonder—even as they braced for whatever **Parallel London** had in store next.

The Globe's wooden echoes faded as a swirl of clockwork light enveloped them, the Orloj's summons drawing them back to the Tower's iron-clad heart.

A distant bell tolled gently, reminding them their final trials lay ahead. Taking a steadying breath, they regrouped and

resumed their path, scanning the **moonlit** streets for the next sign of the **Orloj's** unfolding puzzle.

Chapter 10

Echoes of Loyalty

A **waning** moon cast pale light over **Parallel London,** lamplights floating like will-o'-the-wisps above empty streets. A subtle tension clouded the **Harlequins—Blunt, Checkered, Firee, Reddish, Breezie,** and **Greenie**—as they approached a series of narrow alleyways. Whispers hinted at an elusive mentor, yet no sign or clue revealed itself. **Thumbpee** fidgeted on **Blunt**'s shoulder, while **Buggie** soared in uneasy loops overhead.

"Stay sharp," **Blunt** murmured. "The **Goblin** keeps hinting our **loyalty** will fail. He's trying to sow doubt."

Checkered nodded gravely. "Then we must do the opposite—**trust** each other fully, no matter the **illusions.**"

Yet an eerie hush enveloped the labyrinth of streets, each turn more desolate than the last.

Shadows of Suspicion

Abruptly, a low, spectral voice cut through the silence:

"Extra! Extra! Loyalty lost—secrets uncovered!"

They spun to face a **Dickensian newspaper seller,** transparent and glowing with spectral light. The headlines on his ghostly newspapers flickered and blurred.

Blunt stepped forward cautiously. "Who are you?"

The newspaper seller smiled enigmatically, hollow eyes reflecting faint moonlight.

"Below the city, your answers lie—where **illusions** test faith."

He pointed toward an old underground entrance near **Charing Cross**.

Uncertain glances were exchanged, but the **Harlequins** pressed on. **Firee** forced open a rusted metal gate, stepping into the oppressive darkness of a forgotten **Underground station**. Distant drips echoed like ominous heartbeats; stale air pressed on them.

"Does this not reek of a trap?" **Breezie** whispered, voice trembling slightly.

Reddish steadied her stance, casting a quick look around. "**Loyalty** means we move as one, even if it's risky."

A chilling laugh echoed through the tunnels. In the gloom, the **Dark Goblin** loomed, eyes gleaming with malice. "So, trusting… so easy to divide."

With a snap of his claws, shadowy tendrils lashed out, trying to yank them apart. **Greenie** and **Checkered** nearly lost their grip on each other's hands.

"No!" **Blunt** roared, urging **Firee** to scatter the **Dust of Resolve**. A brilliant aura lit the station, forcing the **Goblin** back with a snarl. "Your **illusions** of discord can't break true **loyalty!**"

Heart hammering, the group dashed deeper into the tunnels, guided now by a faint flicker of torchlight.

A Doorway & an Enigmatic Shop

Soon they entered a hidden chamber where torches flickered on damp stone walls. A humble wooden door stood at the far end, its faded lettering reading:

"Tetrikus Antique Books for the Spirit and the Soul"
(Est. as old as this city is)

Standing defiantly at its entrance was **Paulina Tetrikus**—short yet fierce, eyes flashing green, her presence shaped by life's harsh lessons but tempered with wisdom.

"You're late," she snapped. "The **Goblin** nearly tore you apart by eroding your trust."

Inside, the bookstore felt both cramped and infinite: tall, overstuffed shelves, drifting **magical orbs,** half-open books whose pages glimmered gently. **Paulina** led them along narrow aisles to a circular table piled with three old texts.

"So, you think you understand loyalty?" she asked sharply, her gaze raking over them. "Let me show you how **illusions** can undermine it if you're not vigilant."

"Loyalty," she declared in a clipped, brisk tone, "is not about pleasantries. It's the spine that holds us upright when illusions creep in."

A Trio of Writings: Loyalty vs. Betrayal

At the store's heart lay a **round oak table** with three texts carefully arranged. Paulina lifted the first page:

*

"The Magic in The Light of a New Day"

> *Light of Day,*
> *Light of Life,*
> *Light of Dusk,*
> *Light of Dawn,*
> *Light that shines,*
> *Light that brightens,*
> *Light that each day follows,*
> *"The Circle of Life"*
> *Light that paints life*
> *in a canvas of "Magic Lights"*
> *with a palette of infinite colors,*
> *with endless tones and paint strokes,*
> *Light of Day,*
> *Light of Life,*
> *Light of Dusk,*
> *Light of Dawn.*

*

She read it softly. Paulina's poem unfurled like a banner of fealty, its cadence a heartbeat stitching souls to an unbreakable vow. Finishing, she looked up. **"What does that teach you about loyalty?"**

Breezie frowned. "It's like each new dawn is a chance to reaffirm faith in each other. **If loyalty fails, the light dims for everyone.**"

Paulina nodded. "Yes. Without **loyalty**, the new day's promise is lost. Now…"

She picked up the second piece, titled and started to read earnestly**...**

*

"The Price of Betrayal"

In the heart of the kingdom of Eldoria,
two warriors stood side by side—
Edric and Rowan—
brothers not by blood, but by bond.
From childhood, they had fought together,
defended their king, and sworn an oath:
"Through steel and storm, together we stand."

But as years passed,
greed whispered to Rowan.
He envied Edric's honor,

the trust the king placed in him.

A shadowed figure came one night,

cloaked in darkness,

offering Rowan a deal—

betray Edric,

and the throne's riches would be his.

Temptation won.

On the eve of battle,

Rowan led Edric into an ambush.

The enemies, waiting in silence, struck.

Edric fought, wounded, his strength fading—

yet his eyes never held anger,

only confusion.

"Why?"

he gasped,

before the final blow fell.

With Edric gone,

the kingdom fell soon after.

The army, once unbreakable,

fractured without its most loyal defender.

The enemy stormed the castle,

the king was slain,

and Rowan, believing himself victorious,

claimed his gold.

Yet power built on treachery is fleeting.

The same shadowed figure

who had bribed him came again—

this time with a better offer for another traitor.

Before the night ended,

Rowan lay in the very spot

where he had betrayed his brother.

The kingdom was lost,

not to a mighty army,

but to a single act of disloyalty.

*

A hush followed the final line.

Reddish's voice wavered. "So, a single breach in **loyalty** brought down an entire kingdom…"

Paulina's stern gaze softened slightly. "Yes. Where **loyalty** cracks, illusions of betrayal flourish. Hearts turn, and even the greatest fortress can fall."

Lastly, she lifted the final text:

*

"The Crown of Loyalty"

Loyalty stands, steadfast and true,
A beacon bright in darkest hue.
Through raging storms, through fire's test,
It guards the heart; it knows no rest.

It is the shield, the sword, the vow,
The hand that lifts, the knee that bows.
It does not waver, break, or bend,
It stands with love, defends a friend.

It binds the hearts that time assails,
A whispered oath that never pales.
Empires rise and empires fall,
But loyalty outlives them all.

It is the root of trust so deep,
The promise made, the bond we keep.
It fuels the light in friendship's eye,
A force that gold can never buy.

It is the fire in honor's name,
The guardian of love's great flame.
Through trials fierce and tempests strong,

Loyalty sings an endless song.

It weaves the threads of home and kin,
Where faith endures and peace begins.
It shields the weak, it lifts the lost,
It asks no price; it counts no cost.

It holds the walls when all seems lost,
It warms the soul through winter's frost.
When shadows fall and hope is thin,
Loyalty fights, it does not dim.

No silver tongue, no treacherous snare,
No whispers false, no lies laid bare,
Can shake its might, can make it yield—
For <u>fidelity</u> never leaves the field.

And in the end, when time is done,
When all is dust, when fades the sun,
The names once carved in fleeting stone
Will fall—but <u>loyalty</u> lives on.

*

She closed the booklet gently.

"**Loyalty** is a fortress. Betrayal, once seeded, tears it down.
Now, children: have you truly grasped loyalty's essence?"

Testing Their Trust

Paulina gestured, and the bookstore aisles shifted, forming a **phantasmal corridor** lined with mirrors. Each mirror displayed an image of one Harlequin seemingly plotting behind another's back—whispering secrets, taking advantage. The illusions conjured seeds of suspicion, urging them to question: Is your friend loyal… or about to betray you?

The air thickened as an illusion gripped **Greenie**—a Beirut alley, dust choking her lungs. A childhood friend, Leila, staggered from a bombing's rubble, her voice cracking, "I trusted you!" **Greenie** reached, but Leila turned, fading into smoke.

"You left me," the echo wailed. **Greenie's** knees buckled, tears streaking her face.

"I was scared," she choked out, the memory a knife. **Paulina's** voice cut through, "Loyalty holds when fear screams loudest."

Greenie clenched her fists, whispering, "Not again."

Greenie felt her heart lurch at an illusory scene of Reddish accepting gold to turn on them. Reddish gasped at seeing Blunt forging deals in secret. Fear gripped them.

But **Checkered** inhaled sharply: "No. These images are illusions. *We trust each other.*"

Firee nodded. "We do—**loyalty** is tested in adversity. This is a lie."

In unison, they invoked the bond of friendship. The illusions cracked, revealing only the store's normal aisles. Paulina gave a satisfied half-smile.

"Good. *That* was a taste of how easily betrayal illusions can nudge you into doubt. You overcame by trusting one another. *This* is loyalty at work."

Charm of Fidelity

From a small box, Paulina retrieved a **delicate silver charm** etched with runic symbols. "Here—**The Charm of Fidelity**. Activate it, and the ties among you clarify. Betrayal becomes impossible within your circle; illusions fail to sow suspicion. Use it when illusions or false accusations swirl."

Checkered accepted the charm, feeling a soft hum of unity. The group exhaled collectively, a sense of deeper connection settling over them.

Paulina's gaze turned serious once more. "Remember Eldoria. Betrayal can come from outside or within if you let illusions fester. *Loyalty stands only if each heart defends it.*"

Leaving with Renewed Bonds

Leading them back to the door, Paulina parted with a final admonition: "The Goblin thrives on doubt. If you remain steadfastly loyal, his illusions of betrayal can't take root." Then, with a swirl of lamplight, both the woman and her shop faded into the realm of illusions.

The Harlequins emerged onto a **narrow street**, the faint moon still overhead. The old station behind them now looked sealed and forgotten once more.

A cold gust swept through the courtyard, carrying a distant cackle that faded as quickly as it came, as if the wind mocked their resolve.

Thumbpee hopped impatiently. "You overcame illusions of betrayal… good. But keep that charm close—**the worst illusions are yet to come**."

Exchanging determined nods, they clutched the **Charm of Fidelity**. Their hearts felt fortified by the triple insight of poem, story, and verse. They had glimpsed how betrayal, once unleashed, could annihilate even the mightiest. Yet loyalty's unwavering strength bound them tighter than ever.

With footsteps echoing in quiet resolve, they pressed on into **Parallel London's** moonlit streets, unity shining in each face. The Goblin lurked, illusions lingered, but the Harlequins no longer wavered. For loyalty now echoed in their every breath— **a bond no betrayal could break**.

Foreshadowing Additional Mentors

The illusions parted, *revealing a faint silhouette in the distance—a slender figure with restless movements.*

Reddish (squinting): "Is that… **Morpheus Rubicom**?"

Checkered: **"He's next, I'm sure of it. This can't be a coincidenc**e."

A hush fell, the only sound a low hum of magic in the air. The group prepared to confront the next shepherd-moor, nerves on edge.

Chapter 11

Shadows of Betrayal

A **cold drizzle** cloaked **Parallel London**, turning the city's familiar silhouettes into blurry shapes dripping with gloom. Streetlamps floated overhead like silent sentinels, but their glow felt faint against the oppressive damp. The **Harlequins**—Blunt, Reddish, Checkered, Firee, Breezie, and Greenie—moved cautiously, hearts weighed by a subtle sense of futility. They had endured illusions testing their unity, humility, and loyalty, the **Dark Goblin** loomed still, orchestrating new snares.

"I'm tired," **Breezie** admitted, eyes scanning each alley, voice quivering. "Feels like we can't see an end to this."

Checkered gave a sympathetic nod. "We have come far, but illusions keep multiplying. We can't waver now."

Thumbpee, perched on Blunt's shoulder, folded his small arms. "Surrender's the easiest path for illusions to exploit. You let hopelessness set in, you lose."

Seeds of Doubt

They neared the **Tower of London**, its walls made eerie by the shifting twilight. A swirl of misty illusions danced near the ramparts, conjuring visions of endless corridors. The group braced for illusions but felt a heavy weariness—like each step demanded twice the effort.

Suddenly, an unseen street performer's voice floated through the air:

"Why struggle? This labyrinth of trials will go on forever. There is **no** success. Better to stop now."

For a moment, the Harlequins felt an urge to **simply give in**— why keep going if illusions never ceased?

Blunt gritted his teeth, forcing focus. "No. We can't let illusions coax us into stopping."

Firee nodded, though worry etched his face. "Still, it's like we're stuck in circles, out of breath."

A Perilous Drop

Their moment of indecision let illusions strengthen. **The Dark Goblin** manifested in the gloom, a twisted grin stretching his features. "Ah, your hearts grow weary. Why fight the inevitable? **Quit**."

Shadows fractured the ground beneath them in a sudden quake. **Greenie** and **Reddish** barely caught a slippery ledge, while others clung to crumbling masonry. Water gurgled ominously below. The Goblin's laughter echoed.

"Only fools keep climbing," he jeered, voice thick with malicious glee. "Haven't you realized it's *too hard*?"

A wave of **mental exhaustion** lashed at them, illusions pressing the thought that continuing was *pointless*.

Checkered inhaled sharply. "No! We… must push on!"

Thumbpee barked, "Use your powers—**Dust of Resolve**, now!"

With trembling hands, **Firee** scattered the dust. A glowing aura bathed them, renewing hope and fueling the strength to clamber back onto firm ground. The Goblin snarled in frustration, retreating among swirling shadows.

At the far edge of the courtyard, where illusions had collapsed, a **humble wooden door** flickered into view. Its gilt letters read:

"Rubicom Antiquarian Books about Wealth, Fame, and Love"
(Est. several generations ago)

The group approached warily. They had heard rumors of **Morpheus Rubicom**—the elusive, restless mentor with puffy eyes, a perpetual slouch, and wrangled curls. He was said to disguise himself brilliantly. *Could this be him?*

Encounter with Morpheus Rubicom

Inside, a cramped yet boundless bookstore greeted them. Towers of old tomes stood precariously, illuminated by drifting orbs. At the center paced a **tall, extremely skinny figure**, clothes hanging loosely from his bony frame, curly hair askew, eyes bloodshot with nervous energy. He appeared incapable of sitting still—feet tapping, hands drumming on dusty shelves. With a twitchy half-smile, he greeted them. "**Tenacity**," he murmured. "That's what you lack, yes? Or illusions would never corner you."

Reddish blinked, uncertain. "Are you… Morpheus Rubicom?"

He let out a short, jittery laugh, as if he couldn't help it. "I've been a painter, a musician, a conjurer… but today, yes, Morpheus Rubicom, at your service. Come."

He led them deeper into the shop's winding corridors. A battered sign announced:

"What Is Tenacity to Greatness?"

Two thick manuscripts lay open on a wobbly wooden stand. Surprisingly, the perennially fidgety Rubicom began to recite verses on a paused, pensive tone:

*

"Tenacity"

It's Daring with Grit,

It's "Blunt-Boldness" personified,

It's the "Sharpened-Edginess" of Will,

It's ferociousness and fierceness combined.

It's sinking your teeth,

into anything in life

with the tightest of all strongholds.

It's the Resilient, Unstoppable Drive,

The Relentless Pursuit,

It's the Tell-Tale of Utter and Sheer Determination,

The Ultimate "Fear-Buster,"

An Irrefutable Demonstration of Valor, and Courage,

The Secret-Ingredient to Break-Out of the mold of Conformism,

while Embracing the Unknown.

It's the "Uncontrollable-Impulse"

to seek out, and explore new things,

while calculating the risks.

It's about how good,

the Quality, and Strength

of our Resilience is,

when facing obstacles and challenges.

It's also about how quickly,

we adapt and react to them.

It's always being prepared to Fail,

while ready to Bounce Right-Back,

and continue trying.

Tenacity is the best formula,

to Annihilate and Wipe-Out Uncertainty.

It's one of the most effective methods,

to Dissolve and Erase Anxiety,

leaving no room for it to breathe.

Tenaciousness is a Vital Life-Virtue,

the more we put it into practice,

the more Self-Confidence we acquire,

The more Virtuous Circles,

the more Triumphant-Upward-Spirals

we build,

The better Long-Terms Goals we achieve,

The more Opportunities we seize,

The better Chances to create Innovation,

and Breakthroughs we earn,

Thus, the bigger our Legacy becomes.

Tenacity is the stuff of Wizards,

a Magic Halo,

the one worn by Life Wizards…

"The Wizards of Life."

*

Rubicom's voice quivered with passion, though his frame never ceased its restless movements. Finishing, he peered at them with twitchy intensity. "Harlequins, as opposed to the recklessness of audacity, tenacity often leads to greatness," their restless mentor said unexpectedly yet again, with a calm voice. Then, becoming with usual self he asked animatedly,

"**So?** Why do illusions exploit your exhaustion?"

Breezie swallowed. "Because we forget to keep going, to adapt. When illusions say 'enough,' we freeze."

Rubicom nodded spasmodically, rummaging in a drawer for the second poem. Having found what he was looking for, he extracted a rumpled piece of paper and started to read in earnest:

*

"What is Greatness"

Greatness is the ultimate definition of true success!

Greatness is about the impossible,

Greatness is about the improbable,

Greatness is about,

finding,

tapping,

uncorking,

deploying,

and fully developing,

the awesome, utter, magical power

of our Geniality.

Greatness is achieved through,

the bravest,

fiercest,

most relentless,

ferocious

"Tenacity."

Greatness is,

When you soar above the ordinary,

When you excel against all others,

When you surpass all expectations,

When you go beyond your wildest dreams,

When you achieve

seemingly unsurmountable Goals.

Greatness often takes place as well,

when your creations or accomplishments

universally resonate and propagate

while withstanding the passage of time.

On such cases then,

your greatness is revered,

while becoming ingrained

in society's folklore and culture.

Greatness provides,

the most fulfilling sense of accomplishment,

the intensest,

of all spine tingling's.

The sweetest of all shivering's,

swarming all over your body,

an unstoppable rush of feelings and sensations,

a joyous explosion of our deepest passions,

and the bursting realization,

the deepest satisfaction,

of what is

to triumph,

succeed,

vanquish,

and be victorious.

Greatness and Money are like oil and water,

Material riches never engender Greatness.

Knowledge and experience are key ingredients,

but never the catalysts or clinchers

for greatness.

Greatness does not need

an audience,

recognition,

or accolades.

Authentic greatness takes place within first,

Hence recognition of greatness by others

although carries respect,

it also bears the ballasts of praise and fame,

which are both fickle, and banal.

Therefore, Genuine greatness

is only a manifestation,

of our own inner greatness.

One we are not even aware of,

at first.

Thus, greatness is,

first and foremost

a spiritual manifestation,

an introspective discovery,

an attitude that we wear,

with pride and honor.

Greatness only happens,

when you reach, complete or finish,

your odyssey, your journey, your quest.

Right at that moment.

It's the culmination of a long and arduous climb,

one where we elevate our levels of excellence,

against increasing grades of difficulty

as we navigate through a seemingly

non winnable, endless obstacle course.

Greatness is such memorable instances,

as when you reach the top of a "hill"

and there's no one there.

At the summit of greatness

you are always alone,

simply because no one else has matched,

your feat just yet,

perhaps they'll never do.

There's never an aftermath to Greatness,

as throughout and forever more,

greatness then becomes your credential,

one you'll wear like a badge of honor,

your battle scar,

your rank and file,

your well-deserved proof of ultimate success.

Greatness becomes your persona.

Only those who relentlessly,

dare, chase, persevere, outlast,

and then go where no others are able to,

earn and become bestowed with greatness.

But there is no greatness,

without countless, endless, crushing,

defeats and failures.

Enduring colossal errors, mistakes, setbacks,

while each and every time,

getting back-up,

followed by "going at it,"

again and again...

again and again...,

never, ever giving up.

Foundering is a prerequisite,

an essential building block,

for greatness.

When competing,

Greatness happens,

when with nothing left in the tank

you still reach out for that extra inch,

to cross the finish line ahead of the pack.

Greatness can be,

a circumstance,

a moment,

a pinnacle

or a defeat,

it can be a creation,

in the worlds of art, words, science,

or simply anything competitive in life,

yet always is an accomplishment,

resulting out of an extraordinarily resilient effort.

Greatness is never a happenstance,

but only the result of

unyielding,

disciplined,

unrepentant,

and obsessively-focused-centered will.

Greatness never happens overnight either,

it takes a really long time, to gain it.

Greatness is what moves and advances humanity forward,

by opening new standards and frontiers,

by enriching

our milestones,

treasures,

and legacies.

Greatness is also,

one of the telltales of wizards,

"The Wizards of Life."

*

Closing the text with trembling hands, **Rubicom** asked, **"So, how does unstoppable tenacity breed greatness?"**

Greenie answered softly, "By never giving in, no matter how often illusions or real obstacles knock us down. We keep climbing until we stand on a summit no one else has."

Rubicom's anxious eyes gleamed. "Yes! Greatness, not for glory, but from surpassing each defeat."

Illusory Test: Hall of Half-Defeats

With a jerky wave of one arm, **Morpheus Rubicom** conjured illusions around them—a corridor lined with half-finished attempts and deserted goals. Phantom voices urged them: *You can't complete anything. Why not stop? You always fail anyway.*

The air turned humid, Mumbai's floods rising around **Firee**. His younger brother screamed, trapped as waters surged, but **Firee** froze, caution locking his limbs.

"You didn't move!" the boy cried, sinking. The vision dissolved, leaving Firee gasping, guilt a weight on his chest.

"I couldn't," he muttered, fists clenched.

Morpheus's shadow loomed. "Tenacity acts where doubt paralyzes."

Firee's eyes hardened, the spiral staircase ahead a taunt.

The Harlequins felt self-doubt creep in. But recalling the fervent lines of the "Tenacity" poem, they made themselves try each illusory door.

"Even without magic, mortals climb through despair—wars, losses—tenacity is human," Morpheus said, his gaze piercing the veil of time.

Even when illusions collapsed floors or spawned more shadowy voices, they pressed on, chanting lines from the poems in their minds, forging ahead and finally climbing the circular stairs. Eventually, illusions cracked, revealing the original bookstore.

Rubicom gave a tight-lipped, approving smile, nerves still making him twitch. "You, see? *Tenacity* repels illusions of surrender."

The Sigil of Unyielding Will

He retrieved a **small metallic sigil** shaped like a flame from an old box.

"**Here.** The **Sigil of Unyielding Will**. Invoke it when illusions whisper that you're too tired or powerless. It will stoke your inner fire, banishing the lure of quitting."

Checkered accepted it, sensing a fierce warmth flicker through her. The group exhaled in relief, united by a new reservoir of resolve.

Rubicom's restless gaze darted about. "Do *not* let illusions lull you into complacency. Tenacity must be practiced daily. That's how greatness forms—countless failures, yet you stand again."

A faint shimmer of greenish eyes flickered at the staircase's base, vanishing as Breezie glanced down, leaving only the echo of a patient predator's gaze.

Parting Whispers

Leading them back toward the bookstore entrance, **Morpheus Rubicom** paused, body twitching as if he longed to vanish.

"Remember, illusions prey on *exhaustion*. Keep feeding your determination. *Never* let the Goblin see you hesitate or slump. If you do, illusions will devour your spirit."

Before they could thank him, the bookstore and Rubicom melted into swirling color, leaving them once again in **Parallel**

London's damp street. Distantly, they heard the **Dark Goblin** snarl, thwarted yet again.

Thumbpee hopped on Blunt's shoulder, offering a curt nod.

"Better. Keep that Sigil close."

The Harlequins shared steeled glances; hearts buoyed by the two **poems** still echoing in their minds

"It's sinking your teeth into anything in life…"

"…Greatness is never a happenstance…"

They pressed on through **London's** moonlit drizzle, convinced no illusions of surrender could break them now. For **tenacity** burned in each step—a fierce, unstoppable force that illusions could not hope to quench.

Big Ben's Warning

A deep, resounding toll from Big Ben shook the air, each note reverberating through the Harlequins' chests.

Firee: "That sounded… different. Like a warning."

Greenie: "We're running out of hours. Let's not waste another minute."

They hurried off, uncertain if the Goblin listened from the shadows or if new illusions would strike first.

Chapter 12

The Final Chime

A hush lay over **Parallel London,** its moonlit streets holding their breath as the Harlequins emerged from **Morpheus Rubicom's** elusive bookstore. The drizzling night had turned cold, and in the stillness, every echo of their footsteps felt magnified, each shadow an ominous watcher. Yet the **Sigil of Unyielding Will** glowed faintly in their midst, reminding them of the new tenacity they had forged.

Checkered glanced upward. The moon appeared impossibly large and close, its silvery glow painting the rooftops in spectral light.

"We're so near," she whispered. "The Orloj calls us."

"*But where?*" **Reddish** asked, scanning the deserted alley. In response, a **haunting chime** reverberated gently through the air, tugging them toward a slender passage they had not noticed moments before. The air about it shimmered faintly, hinting that reality itself was bending, beckoning them onward.

"Stay alert," **Blunt** commanded under his breath, heart thrumming. "The Goblin won't let us reach the Orloj unchallenged."

A Flicker of Fear

They ventured into the narrow corridor, each step laden with both dread and resolve. The walls seemed to close in, cobblestones beneath their feet flickering with **enchanted runes** that glowed at the Harlequins' passing. Suddenly, from the darkness ahead came a voice—dry, mocking, steeped in malice.

"You truly believe these *virtues* can save you?" The **Dark Goblin** emerged, twisted figure shimmering with malevolent energy. "The final stroke belongs to me," he hissed. His eyes gleamed with cruel satisfaction.

Firee tensed but forced himself to speak. "Not if we stand together."

The Goblin laughed, a sound cold enough to freeze breath. Shadows erupted like living chains, striking at them from all sides. "Then prove it," he challenged.

Uniting Their Powers

Checkered shouted above the chaos, "Use everything we've gained!"

In a heartbeat, **Breezie** brandished the **Charm of Fidelity**, fortifying their unity. **Greenie** and **Reddish** scattered the **Dust of Resolve**, fueling their courage. Blunt willed the **Mirror of Humility** to reveal the Goblin's illusions, while Firee clutched the new **Sigil of Unyielding Will**, forging an unbreakable drive in their hearts.

A brilliant confluence of light erupted, each virtue—loyalty, perseverance, humility, tenacity—shining as one. The Goblin snarled, forced to recoil by this overwhelming synergy. For an instant, the corridor lit up like midday, the illusions quivering under the combined aura.

"Now," **Blunt** ordered, pressing forward past the momentarily disrupted shadows, leading them into an open courtyard.

Stepping into the Maze Again

Blunt was the first to rouse himself. He stood, shoulders squared with **renewed determination**.

"We have no direct clue, but we know illusions and the Goblin won't wait. Let's be proactive—use the lens the moment something feels off. No more second-guessing."

Checkered lifted her bag, ensuring **Clarity's Lens** was within easy reach.

"Agreed. We can't afford to fumble around any longer."

Greenie and **Firee** exchanged a look of mutual resolve. They quenched their thirst by downing the last of their tea, ignoring the subtle swirl of magical foam at the cup's rim.

All around them, **Parallel London** bustled—a swirl of enthralling chaos. The Harlequins could sense illusions embedded everywhere: a street sign morphing runes under the morning sun, a flamboyant jester conjuring illusions of small phoenixes for giggling passersby. The city was a wondrous tapestry, yet also a labyrinth of potential traps.

Thumbpee fluttered irritably. "Yes, yes, enough chatter. We must go."

A Horizon of Possibilities

Gathering up their belongings, the Harlequins slipped back into the magical streets. The day was just beginning, and so were countless illusions. They knew from experience how easily they could be led astray. Yet the Orloj's words burned in their minds: *Use what you already have. Be decisive. Don't dither.*

Buggie soared ahead, shining small flickers of green light as though scouting for illusions. **Thumbpee** perched on Blunt's shoulder, more watchful than ever. Even the city's hum seemed to intensify, as if acknowledging a silent vow among the six friends.

They might not have a new poem or artifact from the Orloj this time, but they carried the weight of his fatherly warning— a far more pressing impetus than any mere trinket. The Goblin was near, illusions waiting. They would not let confusion or uncertainty undermine them again.

"All right let's do this," Reddish said quietly, her voice laced with confidence. The others nodded. And so, stepping away from the café, they embraced the vibrant, dangerous streets of **Parallel London** once more—ready to prove they could wield their powers with the discipline the Orloj had demanded.

Abbey Road Reverie

They had scarcely settled their thoughts in following Buggie when **Lazarus Zeetrikus**, tall and lanky under his trademark **bent top hat**, materialized from a hazy corner.

"Hurry, young wizards!" he called, voice alive with excitement. **"We're venturing into a more modern era tonight—1960s London, in fact!"**

Before they could question further, he swept them through a **dimly lit** corridor of **Parallel London**, each step dissolving into swirling illusions that brought them to a **tree-lined street** beneath a mild drizzle. Streetlamps cast watery reflections on the pavement, and across the road stood a large white building marked **Abbey Road Studios**.

"We can't be—this is where The Beatles recorded!" gasped **Breezie**, eyes wide with astonishment.

Zeetrikus nodded, pushing open a **shadowy side entrance**. Inside, the corridors felt cramped, mic stands and coiled cables everywhere. A subtle wave of illusions hushed the normal staff—no one saw the **Harlequins** slip into a small control room adjacent to a larger studio.

"Observe quietly," Zeetrikus murmured. **"Music thrives on synergy. Watch these four working as one."**

Behind a **glass partition**, in a softly lit recording space, four young men dressed in **1960s** attire played mid-song, harmonizing a new track. The gentle strum of a guitar and the playful bounce of a bass mingled with a keyboard flourish. Lyrics formed in the hazy studio air, ephemeral text shimmering:

"All you need is love…"

Firee felt an electric thrill spark along her spine.

"This band's music shaped global culture, reaching hearts beyond illusions," she whispered.

Overhead, illusions swirled: glimpses of **iconic album covers** and roaring stadium crowds. A fleeting image of a bespectacled musician, one who **left us too soon**, flickered like a wistful afterimage—his **dream of a world united** living on through a **tender** ballad about imagining borders erased, illusions undone, and souls unchained by fear.

"See how they fuse each chord," Zeetrikus noted, tipping his **top hat. "Each contribution shapes the masterpiece. Britain's cultural legacy isn't merely classical or ancient— its modern creations also transform our world."**

From behind the mixing console, a recording engineer signaled a restart. The synergy intensified—**the quartet** exchanged grins, weaving a harmonic tapestry that would echo in countless futures.

Greenie exhaled softly; her eyes misty. **"They're just four friends, and yet they redefined an era."**

Zeetrikus returned her gaze with a slight nod. **"Indeed. As the Orloj reminded you—*illusions fade, but creativity endures*. The power of imagination can outlast any darkness."**

The lights in the studio flickered as **Zeetrikus** opened another **portal**, swirling with

subtle starlight and the faint notes of a **timeless** melody. **"Never forget,"** he said gently. **"A single chord or lyric can ripple through decades, bridging illusions of strife with harmonies of hope…just as a certain ballad might ask us to 'imagine' a world without boundaries or fear."**

Imagine…

It was as if a quiet echo of a later **song** hovered among them— a melody from a time beyond the band's earliest hits. A gentle acoustic piano chord drifted through the illusions, weaving into the track still playing in the real studio below.

Reddish brushed at a sudden lump in her throat. **"He wrote that, didn't he?** A different moment in time but still a dream of unity—of illusions undone by love and peace."

Zeetrikus—noting the shift in the illusions—inclined his **bent top hat** sadly. **"Yes.** That dreamer's message soared even after tragedy struck. It reminds us that illusions of fear and distrust can be dispelled if we dare to see ourselves as one people, one world."

For an instant, the ephemeral text glowed brighter:

"…You may say I'm a dreamer…"

Checkered exhaled softly, placing a hand on **Firee**'s shoulder. **"Perhaps that's our calling too?** As wizards, we face illusions daily. If a single lyric can shift hearts, surely our magic can bring people closer?"

Blunt managed a wistful smile. **"He imagined a borderless world—a place free from illusions that divide.** Our quest is not so different."

Returning Through the Portal

A gentle tug of magic enveloped them. One by one, the **Harlequins** stepped through the **portal**, leaving the hum of **1960s** studio equipment for the **shadowy** hush of **Parallel London's** present. The drizzle persisted, pattering on cobblestones, but now a renewed warmth pulsed in their chests.

They found themselves back at the **moonlit** corner where **Zeetrikus** had first whisked them away—near a quiet intersection of old brick buildings. Though no immediate illusions stirred, they felt the lingering resonance of that legendary session.

"That synergy," Checkered said, brushing water droplets from her sleeve. **"It echoes the Orloj's advice about unity and swift action. Each wizard in tune, no hesitation."**

Zeetrikus, perched at the threshold of a dim corridor, gave a final wave of his **bent top hat. "Music or magic—each chord or spell demands the same harmony of purpose. Let's keep moving. Our next challenge awaits."**

And with that, he vanished into the gently swirling air, leaving the **Harlequins** to exchange determined smiles. In unspoken agreement, they pressed on toward the next **twist** in the Orloj's labyrinth, hearts brimming with the enduring lesson of a **band** whose songs transcended illusions—and a fervent hope that one day, all might heed the message:

"All you need is love… Imagine… a world free from the illusions that divide us."

A Sudden Summons

A faint glow pulsed along the alleyway, forming an ethereal arrow in midair.

Checkered (raising eyebrows): "An arrow… from the Orloj or another trick?"

Reddish: "Only one way to find out. We follow or we lose more time."

They exchanged determined looks, stepping forward, the arrow brightening ominously as if beckoning them into unknown depths.

The Orloj's Final Hour

There, in silent splendor, stood the **Orloj** itself—an **enormous astronomical clock** ringed by shifting runes and faint, ghostly gears spinning high in the sky.

The **clock face** loomed, its dials set to a minute before midnight, each **tick** resonating like an ancient heartbeat. Symbols for the zodiac, planets, and arcane sigils glowed in the gloom. Suddenly, the courtyard trembled—**the Goblin** reappeared, furious, his shape enlarging with every ragged breath.

"You cannot escape *fate*!" he shrieked, hurling dark illusions that rippled like black flames. The Harlequins braced themselves, shoulders squared, their newly enhanced powers at the ready.

The Dark Goblin loomed, his voice a jagged blade. "I trusted once—your precious bond will shatter as mine did under Prague's gears." His claws slashed, but the Harlequins stood firm, their unity a shield. His illusions flickered, faltering, and a vision bled through unbidden—a younger Goblin, cloaked in Orloj runes, pleading as a clock tower buckled.

"Don't leave me!" he cried, but his friends faded, their backs turned. The stones crushed him, darkness seeping into his screams. Greenie gasped,

"He was like us." Blunt's sword wavered, "Could we have saved him?" The Orloj's voice rumbled, steady and final, "His choice was his own."

The Goblin snarled, "Unity… lies…" as his form frayed, disintegrating into ash. His wail lingered, a mournful thread in the silence.

Checkered slumped against a gear, her breath ragged. "I thought we'd break this time," she whispered, hands trembling.

Breezie traced a scar from Paris along his arm, faint but sharp. "Almost did," he said, voice low. The silence stretched, heavy with the fight's cost.

Firee stared at the ash where the Goblin fell, Greenie's eyes still wet. Big Ben's hum pulsed through them, a slow heartbeat syncing their breaths.

Blunt clenched his fists, "We're still here."

The Tower loomed, its call sharper now.

Above them, **the Orloj** chimed, the **final stroke** echoing through their minds. A **powerful wave** pulsed out from the clock's face, enveloping the Harlequins in a protective halo of radiance. Time seemed to slow, each breath elongated, each heartbeat thrumming in perfect unison.

"You have come far, young ones," a gentle, fatherly voice boomed from nowhere and everywhere at once. **"This Goblin feeds on doubt—yet you have the courage born of your journey's virtues. Stand firm."**

That warmth of the Orloj's presence—so paternal, so **immeasurably ancient**—bolstered their spirits. In that brief, victorious quiet, a sinister rumble rattled through the air, shaking the gears and stones around them. The Harlequins froze, their gazes snapping back toward the scattering ash. It coalesced violently, shadows pulling together into a twisted silhouette, deeper and more formidable than before. Eyes flared crimson, burning with renewed malevolence.

"You dare celebrate too soon," hissed the Goblin, voice rippling with rage, distorted as if wrenched from a void. He surged upward, growing rapidly, his form writhing with tendrils of shadow and streaks of crimson lightning.

Checkered stumbled backward, raising a hand instinctively. "He's stronger than ever—"

The Goblin roared, an earsplitting cacophony of despair, doubt, and fury combined. Shadows whipped forward, enveloping the courtyard in choking darkness. The protective radiance of the Orloj flickered momentarily, its ancient strength tested by the Goblin's ferocity.

"Your unity is brittle!" the Goblin bellowed, eyes narrowing to slits of fire. "I will shatter it, piece by fragile piece."

Breezie staggered, hands clutching at his chest, breath stolen by the oppressive darkness. Firee reached out blindly, seeking the others, her voice tight. "Hold… hold together!"

Greenie's eyes flashed defiantly through tears, his voice cutting sharply through the Goblin's maelstrom. "No! Our bond is forged by every challenge we've faced. We won't be broken now!"

Blunt roared, surging forward into the darkness, Thumbpee gripping his shoulder tightly. "Stand strong—remember the virtues that brought us here!"

Checkered inhaled deeply, stepping forward. "Our unity is stronger than your darkness," she declared to the Goblin.

Lights swirled and flared, each Harlequin's color merging into a singular, pulsating brilliance. The Goblin howled, fighting to keep his illusions intact. But the synergy of discipline, loyalty, kindness, humility, perseverance, and tenacity fused with the Orloj's paternal aura was too much. Once again, the **Dark Goblin** crumbled, then disintegrated into swirling blackness, banished—for now; a requiem of ash and echoes, his malice swallowed by the chime of unity's dawn.

With a restless laugh, he motioned them through an iron door—proving that in the face of the Goblin's final attempt at crushing their spirits, their tenacity shone unbreakable. In silent splendor, stood the Orloj—the enormous astronomical clock ringed by shifting runes and faint, ghostly gears spinning high in the sky.

The iron door led them upward through twisting stone, the air growing crisp as they breached the Tower's heights, stepping into an open courtyard where the Orloj awaited once more.

A Moment of Triumph

Silence fell, broken only by the Orloj's **resonant ticking**. The Harlequins, breathless and awed, sensed the magnitude of their victory. Though they knew the Goblin might survive in some distant shadow, this confrontation was **the** test of everything they had learned.

Checkered exhaled, voice trembling with relief. "We did it."

Reddish nodded, though caution shadowed his eyes. "But the Orloj's final challenge… it's not over, is it?"

Greenie gazed up at the towering clock face, thoughtful certainty in his eyes. "Midnight approaches. From the Orloj's words and the path we've traveled, it's clear: our last trial awaits at the Tower of London. We have only hours left in this realm."

At that, the Orloj's voice returned, quieter but no less paternal:

"Yes, dear Harlequins—your final test stands beyond these illusions. Go forth with the virtues that have shaped you."

The clock's hands crept toward midnight, gears whirring in subtle unison. Another chime rang softly, **affirming** their readiness.

Blunt lifted his chin resolutely. "We face the Tower of London next. Let's not falter."

Thumbpee, perched again on Blunt's shoulder, gave a gruff nod. "No time to waste. Move out."

Onward to the Tower

Thus, the Harlequins stepped away from the Orloj's courtyard, hearts thudding with renewed fervor. They had repelled the Goblin's illusions, united all their powers. Yet a final confrontation still lay before them—**the ultimate test** that would determine whether they could indeed ascend beyond their **Master Wizardry** into the Orloj's highest calling.

As they exited the courtyard, the Orloj's bright aura faded to a gentle glow, as though offering silent encouragement. The city's gloom pressed in once more, but the Harlequins no longer feared it. For they carried the Orloj's fatherly blessing, their virtues shining as a shield none of the Goblin's illusions could shatter.

CHAPTER 13

The Tower of London Challenge

"At last," **Blunt** murmured, gazing at the **Tower**'s silhouette.

"We're here," **Checkered** whispered back, her eyes alight with anticipation.

They had come full circle—**Venice**, **Prague**, **Paris**—all culminating in this night within the **Tower of London**. And now, standing amid moonlit cobblestones and the ancient fortress walls, the six **Young Wizards** felt **time** quiver around them.

No swirling gondolas or effervescent Eiffel illusions this time—only the dark, historic gravitas of the **Tower**, centuries of intrigue whispering in every stone. Lightning flickered over distant ramparts, followed by rolling thunder. Something vast and magical was about to happen.

The Gathering at the Tower

The **Harlequins**—**Blunt**, **Reddish**, **Checkered**, **Firee**, **Greenie**, and **Breezie**—approached the **Tower**'s outer gate, expressions set with both caution and excitement. This final trial would determine whether they ascended to **Orloj**

Wizards—a rank beyond **Master Wizards**, rumored to wield even greater temporal and moral magic.

Two tiny figures hovered overhead**, Thumbpee**, perched on **Blunt**'s shoulder, arms crossed, eyes darting for threats; **Buggie**, looping in tight circles, bright wings leaving a faint greenish trail.

"We're ready," **Checkered** said, recalling how close they had come to failure in earlier quests.

Thumbpee nodded, his squeaky voice serious. "Each time, you overcame illusions by living your virtues. Tonight, you face six fresh trials, each tied to the flaw or virtue you learned. Fail even one, and the path to Orloj Wizardry collapses."

No one spoke, but their resolve shimmered. Beyond the gate, **ravens** cawed, as though the Tower's legendary guardians were sounding an alarm.

Buggie's wings glowed bright. "Follow," he buzzed, shining a tiny green beam at a

massive wooden door set into the stone. Together, they stepped through the threshold.

An Unexpected Welcome

They emerged into a wide courtyard overshadowed by the **Tower**'s central keep. Dark shapes flitted from parapet to parapet above. Torches sputtered in iron brackets, the interplay of shadow and flame lending the fortress an otherworldly air.

Suddenly, six columns of pale light formed around them, coalescing into six separate illusions—each the spindly shape of a **mentor** they knew so well: **Cornelius Tetragor**, in voluminous white robe and trailing beard**, Lettizia Dillettante**, statuesque and Nordic, arms folded in quiet pride**, Lazarus Zeetrikus**, top hat bent at an odd angle**, Lucrecia Van Egmond**, tall and pale, hair threaded with moonlight**, Paulina Tetrikus**, short, intense, ever so quick-tempered**, and Morpheus Rubicom**, clothes too large, pacing restlessly.

All at once, they spoke in unison:

"Harlequins! Tonight, you challenge the Tower. To become Orloj Wizards, you must conquer six trials. We appear here only as illusions, each testing the flaw or virtue we taught. Illusions swirl like fog. Use your powers—yet moral choice is your greatest weapon. Good luck."

In a blink, the illusions vanished. From overhead, the great clock of the Tower's chapel (silent by mortal standards) began tolling softly in the **Harlequins'** minds—an echo of the **Orloj's** mystical presence.

Breezie exhaled. "We'd better expect illusions around every turn."

Blunt nodded. "No sense waiting."

They crossed to the inner gate, unlatched it, and disappeared into the **Tower's** depths.

In a dimly lit corridor preceding the final chamber, the floor morphed into shards of ice, while columns of flame roared from iron grates. The Goblin's voice echoed, "So you think your meager feats can withstand a real test?"

Greenie felt a wave of panic as the cold nipped her ankles, but **Checkered** squeezed her shoulder reassuringly.

"We've walked through worse. Remember Prague?"

United, the Harlequins advanced. The illusions parted like a curtain of sparks and snowdrifts. Their bodies remained unburned; their feet uncut. In moments, they were beyond the gauntlet, hearts pounding—but unscathed. A testament to their earliest lessons.

The Test of Generosity
The Labyrinth of Crowns

Inside the **Tower**'s lower hall, dim torchlight revealed a broad corridor lined with dusty relics—historical weapons, battered suits of armor, tattered tapestries. Suddenly, a swirling glow ignited on the floor, forming a golden spiral leading to a side chamber.

They followed it into a vaulted room. Display cases stood open, each containing a crown or scepter, glittering with jewels. An unsettling aura surrounded these treasures.

Greenie gasped. "Are these illusions of the Crown Jewels…?"

A voice echoed from the gloom:

"Take your prize, young wizards. Haven't you earned a reward?"

The swirling glow around the treasure brightened, pulling them in. A hush fell.

Reddish frowned. "Something's…off."

Checkered nodded. "If we're here to prove ourselves, grabbing this loot feels wrong."

But the corridor behind them sealed abruptly with a clang. The only visible exit was a tall door on the opposite side, locked beneath a golden crest.

The Allure of Treasure

Flickers of illusions danced among the jewels:

- A golden orb shimmered at **Firee**, promising unstoppable power.

- A diamond-encrusted dagger winked at **Breezie**, tempting double agility.

- A legendary scepter seemed to beckon **Blunt**: Take me, you deserve it.

The illusions whispered, **"You've done so much—why not claim what's owed?"**

Greenie's breath caught. "This is the first trial. If we give in to greed—"

"—we fail at **Generosity**," **Blunt** finished.

Illusions pressed harder, voices overlapping: Take one treasure… No one will know…

Reddish set her jaw. "We share everything, or we walk away."

"For them, always," Reddish whispered, her defiance now love the trial's gold glowing brighter.

Act of Generosity

Approaching a battered chest in the center, they saw a small golden bowl, free of illusions, bearing a simple inscription:

"GIVE OF YOURSELF WHAT YOU COVET MOST."

Firee placed a hand over her heart. "Something symbolic. We each must offer something we hold dear."

Without hesitation, each dropped in a cherished item, **Blunt** removed a ring given by a beloved mentor, **Checkered** parted with her prized silver charm, **Reddish** offered a treasured heirloom pin, **Breezie** placed a meaningful black-and-white wristband, **Firee** relinquished a battered pocket watch from home, and **Greenie** set down her beloved pen for journaling magic.

At once, illusions around the jewels flickered and dissolved. The chest glowed; the locked door's crest unlatched.

A swirl of smoke revealed **Cornelius Tetragor:** "**Generosity** in the face of temptation—well done, Harlequins. True wealth lies not in hoarding but in giving."

He bowed, then vanished. The door swung open into the next corridor.

The Test of Arrogance
The Mirror Corridor

A winding passage led them through the White Tower's interior, merging into an opulent corridor lined with tall, polished mirrors. Moonlight from high windows caused reflections to shift wildly, creating a disorienting hall of infinite images.

The mirror double sneered, its face twisting into a shadowed Notre-Dame spire. "You nearly lost them in Paris—your orders faltered, and **Firee** paid the price."

Blunt's breath hitched as an illusion flared: **Firee,** limp, a jagged wound from a falling gargoyle staining his cloak red. His friends' accusing eyes bored into him—**Greenie's** tears, **Reddish's** snarl. His hands trembled, gripping at the Tower's stone.

"I led us wrong," he rasped, voice breaking. The double laughed,

"You're nothing alone."

Blunt's gaze found his Harlequins, real and unbroken, beyond the glass.

"I'm nothing without you all," he whispered, raw and unguarded. The mirror shattered, his humility a quiet roar, dissolving the lie. As the trial faded, he murmured,

"Failure's my shadow, but you're my light."

Reddish exhaled. "We've dealt with mirror illusions before—stay sharp."

As they entered, each mirror's surface rippled, spitting out life-sized copies of the **Harlequins**, postures warped by arrogance and vanity, **Blunt**'s double smirked, adjusting imaginary medals: "I alone am the leader—this quest would be nothing without me," **Firee**'s double insisted her caution was the only thing saving the group, **Checkered**'s double claimed she handled the hardest tasks alone…and so on.

Battling the Ego

These false reflections advanced, mocking them, each proud clone trying to overshadow the real wizard. The corridor's mirrors vibrated ominously, forcing each Harlequin to confront their vain counterpart.

Greenie found her clone boasting about unstoppable intuition, belittling others. Furious, she lunged, but anger only fed the illusions.

Breezie realized direct magical blasts scattered harmlessly. Ego illusions thrived on negativity.

In **thought-communication, Checkered** shouted:

"Everyone—**humility**! If we feed them pride, they grow. We must do the opposite."

One by one, each wizard faced their mirror self with humble truths, **Blunt**: "I rely on my friends. Alone, I'd fail," **Reddish**: "I need their perspectives. My boldness alone isn't enough," **Greenie**: "My intuition is stronger with everyone's input."

As each declared humility, the respective pride-clone cracked and dissolved into shards of light. Echoes of mocking laughter died away.

Mentor's Approval

From behind a mirror stepped **Lettizia Dillettante**, arms folded over her Nordic frame, expression calm yet proud:

"Well done. **Arrogance** is sly—praise can twist swiftly into ego. You overcame by embracing humility. Remember, the surest defense against pride is trusting each other's strengths."

She nodded, then vanished in swirling dust. The corridor door creaked open. They pressed on.

The Test of Kindness (Flaw: Callousness)
The Ghostly Prisoners

They next emerged into a dismal prison block, stone cells on either side. The Tower's history as a place of confinement pressed upon them. Torchlight flickered across rusted iron bars.

A plaintive cry rose from a nearby cell: "Help…someone…"

Approaching cautiously, they spied a half-transparent spectral figure inside, slumped behind heavy bars. The door was locked tight.

Greenie frowned. "We must do something."

"I see you now," **Breezie** murmured to the spectral prisoners, his touch soft, redeeming the past with quiet grace.

Buggie hovered, shining a small beam at an ancient lock. But the moment **Firee** tried an unlocking charm, more ghosts appeared in adjacent cells, moaning pitifully—far too many to free one by one.

Checkered whispered, "Is this an illusion testing whether we'll bother with strangers' suffering?"

Compassion Beyond Logic

As they hesitated, the moaning swelled, intangible hands reaching from cells, fueling dread. **Reddish** and **Breezie** began opening locks, but for every freed ghost, more manifested.

Time was short. Could they help them all? **Blunt** realized:

"**Kindness** isn't about fixing everything. It's about caring enough to try."

So, they offered small mercies: consoling words, illusions of warmth, gentle blessings. Even if they couldn't save every specter physically, they refused to be callous. Gradually, the ghosts' wails diminished, illusions fading cell by cell.

Soon, the passage stood empty except for a single battered door at the far end.

Mentor's Cameo

From the shadows materialized **Lazarus Zeetrikus**, top hat askew, relief tempering his usual sternness:

"**Kindness** given freely—without guarantee of success. Well done, Harlequins. Compassion stands even when the cause seems hopeless. Press on."

They thanked him softly. He vanished, allowing them to pass into the next tower chamber.

The corridor sloped downward, water rising with each step until it surged at their chests. Through the gloom, illusions of drowning forms bobbed eerily.

Firee swallowed hard. "Anyone else suspect this is more than a trick?"

"We can handle it," said **Breezie**, recalling their **breathing underwater** power from Venice. One by one, they slipped beneath the surface, illusions swirling around them like ghostly kelp.

Holding hands for support, the Harlequins calmly traversed the submerged hallway, illusions shrieking at their effortless composure. Emerging breathless but alive, they pressed on, refusing to let the Goblin's final traps deter them.

The Test of Perseverance
The Armory of Fatigue

They entered a large circular chamber lined with ancient armaments—swords, spears, crossbows displayed in neat rows. At once, a crushing aura of weariness set in, a mental heaviness that whispered stop trying, it's too hard.

Checkered rubbed her temples. "Why do I suddenly feel drained?"

Every breath deepened their exhaustion. A subtle enchantment in the air urged them to throw down wands, to rest, to admit defeat.

Reddish found her knees wobbling, as though climbing another step was impossible. **Breezie** nearly dropped the lens out of sheer apathy.

Facing the Urge to Quit

A swirl of illusions formed monstrous shapes that advanced not with fury but with a slow, relentless push—like an unwinnable slog. **Blunt** tried hurling a basic stun spell, but his arm felt like lead. The illusions fed on the group's sagging determination.

"Don't...give...in," **Greenie** gasped. "**Perseverance** is pushing through."

"I finish what I start," Checkered snarled, pushing past, her resolve steel where doubt once cracked.

One beast slithered close, entangling **Firee**'s ankles in illusions of futility: Why bother? You'll never finish…

Holding On

They closed ranks, recalling how discipline and impetus ignited perseverance. Each wizard forced a step forward, **Reddish** repeated, "We keep going. We've come so far," **Checkered** locked eyes with **Blunt**.

"No illusions can outrun our will," **Breezie** mustered a final spark of energy: "We stand. We do not yield."

As they collectively refused to quit, the illusions shriveled. The oppressive heaviness lifted. The monstrous shapes faded, leaving the stone armory silent.

Lucrecia Van Egmond emerged behind a battered rack of halberds, her pale hair and milky eyes reflecting quiet pride:

"You overcame the temptations of giving up. **Perseverance** triumphs where the will to continue is tested hardest. Well done, dear Harlequins."

She bowed, and the next chamber door opened.

The Test of Loyalty
The Tower Raven Keeper

At a rusted iron gate deep in the Tower's labyrinth, a spectral guard hovered, demanding credentials. "None shall pass without the official seal."

Reddish grinned slyly. "We can…improvise." She invoked **shapeshifting**, adopting the guard's own uniformed appearance. The illusions flickered, trying to trap her in that form, but she steeled her mind.

Slipping through the gate, she placed a palm on the sigil. The bolts clicked, illusions trembling in fury. Hastily, **Reddish** resumed her normal shape before the illusions could lock it forever. The door swung open, freeing the group to advance.

Pressing onward, they found themselves in a broader courtyard overshadowed by Byward Tower.

A stooped **Raven Keeper** in ragged uniform beckoned them, ravens perched along a wooden rail.

"I need help," he rasped. "The Tower's caretaker deserted me. Will you stand by me, or leave me to toil alone?"

Thunder rumbled overhead. **Midnight** loomed closer—time was slipping away. Could they spare a moment for someone else's troubles?

Breezie hesitated. "We're short on time. Is this an illusion or a genuine request?"

Checkered cast a glance at the gloom. "But if we walk away, we fail **loyalty**—we pledged to help those we meet."

Standing by Another

Steeling themselves, they approached. The keeper pointed to tasks neglected: feeding ravens, securing gates, mending a fence. The illusions layered in glimpses of betrayal—images of past wizards who walked away from burdens.

Yet the Harlequins chose unity, **Blunt** quickly refilled feed troughs, **Reddish** hammered loose boards, and **Greenie** soothed unsettled birds, everyone pitched in, refusing to abandon the keeper's needs.

Sweat beaded on brows, precious minutes ticked by, but they stayed.

The Raven Keeper morphed into Leila's pleading face. "I won't abandon anyone again," Greenie sobbed, sealing the trial. "Trust is my strength now," she breathed, victorious. When the final task finished, the keeper lifted his cloak— revealing **Paulina Tetrikus** with a slightly mischievous smile. They almost overlooked her at first, for the top of her head reached only to Checkered's shoulder. Short, slightly hunched, and perpetually frowning, Paulina fixed them with green eyes as vivid as emerald embers. Her short black hair framed a face that could have been beautiful if not for the deep crease of frustration across her brow.

Even as she spoke, she avoided prolonged eye contact, as though too proud—or too furious—to acknowledge them fully. "Well, well… you didn't run. **Loyalty** means standing by allies, even in inconvenience. The Goblin can't sow betrayal if your bond is unshakable."

Without warning, she tilted her chin high to meet Reddish's gaze, scowling up at the taller girl. "If you betray even one friend," she spat, "the whole chain breaks. Trust is not repaired so easily." Then, in the same breath, she softened just enough to add: "Stay close, or risk falling apart."

She vanished in a swirl of feathers. **Buggie** hummed triumphantly, guiding them forward.

The Test of Tenacity

The Spiral Staircase of Futility

A stone arch led them into the **White Tower's** central keep. A **spiral staircase** coiled upward, seemingly infinite, but **illusions** flickered at every step. Unlike the earlier trials of perseverance, here the illusions whispered of **utter futility**—that climbing higher was pointless, that **giving up** would be easier.

Reddish felt her stomach twist. "Another climb? What now?" **Firee** grimaced. "The **Goblin** insisted we'd lose heart eventually. Maybe this is his final push to make us surrender."

They ascended. Each step revealed phantom images of themselves giving up on past challenges—abandoning friends halfway, turning from obstacles in exhaustion. At times, the illusions hissed:

"Why keep going? Enough is enough. No one will blame you for quitting."

Rejecting Resignation

Breezie paused, shaken by a vision showing him collapsing in defeat, illusions chanting that he'd done enough. "That's not me. I've never walked away like that."

Greenie placed a gentle hand on his arm. "We trust you to keep going. Let's not surrender so close to the end."

"I won't hesitate again!" **Firee** roared, clawing up the endless stairs, breaking free. "Action's my fire now," he panted, triumphant.

Whenever the illusions conjured a scenario of **resignation**, another Harlequin invoked their newly honed **tenacity**—remembering how they had learned never to yield to despair. These illusions grew frustrated each time, outraged they could not break the group's will.

Step by labored step, the **Harlequins** climbed beyond the illusions, unwavering in their determination. Their refusal to **give up** banished every false scenario of hopelessness.

Final Mentor & Door

At last, they reached a **final landing**, facing an ornate **black-iron door.**

Morpheus Rubicom appeared—tall, puffy-eyed, nervous energy crackling around him: "You overcame the illusions of complete **resignation. Tenacity** holds firm when every muscle and thought urges you to quit. **Congratulations**, dear Harlequins."

With a restless laugh, he motioned them through the iron door—proving that in the face of the Goblin's final attempt at crushing their spirits, their **tenacity** shone unbreakable.

The Tower's ravens croaked, "Beware the axe, beware the crown," their feathers glinting with spectral Tudor roses, echoes of Anne Boleyn's doom.

The Final Induction

They stepped into a high chamber near the Tower's top. Wind roared through shattered windows, offering a breathtaking view of London's night skyline. The Tower sang, its spire piercing fate, their triumph a constellation born from the dust of conquered flaws. **Big Ben** glowed faintly in the distance, a subtle reminder of the **Orloj**'s hidden presence.

At the chamber's center stood the **Orloj** in broad-shouldered human form, mustache bristling, arms folded in fatherly pride. **Thumbpee** and **Buggie** flanked him, looking inordinately pleased.

The Orloj's voice softened, warm as a hearth at dawn. "You've grown, my children," it murmured, a fatherly timbre replacing its earlier sternness—stern as a judge at midnight—from their first meeting.

"You have proven yourselves beyond **Master Wizards**—tonight, you become **Orloj Wizards**."

His eyes gleamed with ancient wisdom. "Your final 24 hours of illusions are done. Each challenge tested you deeply, yet you overcame. You bested **greed with generosity**, **pride with humility**, **callousness with kindness**, **giving up with perseverance**, and two forms of **disloyalty** with unbreakable loyalty."

A swirl of starlight enveloped the six young wizards. Ephemeral runes glowed on their harlequin suits—**symbols of time and balance**, the Orloj's hallmark.

"Wear these proudly," the Orloj rumbled, "as reminders that virtue powers your magic. You are guardians of temporal harmony. Step forth and claim your new rank."

He lifted both hands. A cascade of molten gold surged through their souls, each rune a heartbeat of eternal chimes, an electric surge—new layers of magic unfurling. As the runes flared, a faint echo whispered through Big Ben —"Unity… lies…"—the Goblin's last cry, haunting their triumph with a shadow of what might have been.

They were **Orloj Wizards** now, entrusted to safeguard the delicate interplay of virtues and time.

Exhausted and exhilarated, they exchanged awed smiles.

"Remember," the Orloj said gently, "this is no end, but a beginning. Darkness may test you again. Keep these virtues close."

Dawn over the Thames

In a final swirl of power, the Tower chamber dissolved into morning light. The six Harlequins blinked as they emerged by the fortress gates, **exhausted yet triumphant**. Crisp birdsong cut through the hush—**the city stirring to a new day**, unaware of the illusions that had twisted through the night.

The midnight sky swirled above the fortress, where the moon cast silver light across the worn ramparts. Inside the highest chamber of the Tower of London, Blunt and his five fellow Harlequins—Reddish, Firee, Checkered, Breezie, and Greenie—stood in reverent silence. They had just earned the highest honor of their magical journey: **Orloj Wizardry**.

A gentle breeze stirred, swirling away the final vestiges of illusion.

The Tower of London

The Tower's ghostly guardians—ravens and ancient spirits—seemed to bow in acknowledgment. At the center of the chamber stood **Kraus**, the wise antiquarian who had guided them through so many twists. His eyes shone with approval.

"All is quiet," Checkered breathed, gazing at their newly earned insignias glowing softly on their harlequin suits.

Firee swallowed. "So…this is it? We're—"

"Indeed," Kraus finished for her, voice warm with pride. "You are Orloj Wizards now, guardians of the clock's deeper mysteries. But your journey in this realm is done for now. Time draws short. You must return to your world."

Far below, the Tower's floors resonated with a soft hum, the last echoes of Parallel London's magic beginning to recede. Blunt cast one final look over the roofline, glimpsing faint, ephemeral gears turning in the sky—a reminder that the Orloj still watched over them.

Kraus placed a hand upon the ancient stones. "We must hurry. The door between worlds will close soon. The city's illusions have dissolved, and if you linger, you risk being trapped here until the next cycle."

Thumbpee and **Buggie**—the Orloj's diminutive sons—fluttered by the window, their small forms haloed in moonlight. They, too, felt the pull of finality.

"All right," Blunt said, steadying his voice though his heart thumped with emotion. "Where do we cross back?"

Kraus touched a section of wall. At once, the stones rippled like water, revealing a portal swirling in softly lit patterns. "Not Big Ben this time—your chaperones wait where you left them. The portal leads us to **York Minster**, where only moments have passed for them, even though you've spent a full day in Parallel London."

Greenie's eyes shone with excitement and a tinge of sadness. "I'll miss this place," she murmured. "Despite its dangers, it's…magical."

With gentle laughter, Kraus ushered them forward. "All your new powers remain with you. Whenever the Orloj calls again, you'll be ready."

And so, with final backward glances at the rapidly fading Tower's ancient walls, the six new Orloj Wizards stepped through the portal—leaving behind the moonlit illusions and swirling energies of Parallel London.

Return to York Minster

The air shimmered, and they staggered onto the worn stone floor of a side chapel in York Minster. Ghostly echoes of the centuries-old building surrounded them: tall stained-glass windows, candlelit alcoves, and the distant murmur of the city at night.

Blinking in the sudden stillness, they spotted **Bart Sutton-Leigh** and **Antonella Cromwell-Smith**—Blunt's aunt and uncle—exactly where they had parted from them less than half an hour ago. The adults had been in a subtle, dreamlike daze, as though the few minutes had stretched into hours of quiet. The moment the Harlequins appeared, Bart and Antonella awoke fully, startled but smiling.

"Blunt!" Bart exclaimed, rushing forward. "You're—back. But how—?"

Antonella peered at them, relief flooding her features. "We lost track of you for a moment. Are you all right?"

"We only turned a moment—where have you been?" Bart exclaimed, voice unsteady with both concern and awe.

Blunt mustered a tired grin, stepping closer to Antonella and Bart, whose **relief** was almost palpable. "We'll explain… some of it," he said softly, the **weight of secret trials** behind his words.

Reddish exchanged relieved looks with Breezie. "We're fine. A bit tired, but…we did it."

The others stifled laughter, for "a bit tired" barely described their marathon of illusions and perils. Still, they couldn't reveal every detail—the adults only vaguely sensed that extraordinary magic had just transpired.

Kraus stepped out of the portal last, giving the chaperones a respectful nod. "Time can be peculiar in these old cathedrals," he said mysteriously. "They've returned safely, exactly as promised."

Bart and Antonella cast unsure smiles. Although uncertain of the exact truths behind Kraus's words, they felt a gentle assurance that all was well. The portal behind him flickered, then vanished into the gloom, sealing the realm of Parallel London behind them.

A New Horizon (in York)

Moonlight streamed through York Minster's lofty stained glass, bathing the group in colorful patterns. The six friends gathered close, hearts brimming with accomplishment.

"So, we're… Orloj Wizards now," Checkered murmured, testing the phrase on her tongue.

"Yes," Firee confirmed, face glowing. "We carry these powers and responsibilities forever."

Greenie turned to Kraus. "Thank you—for guiding us here and back."

Kraus bowed slightly, the corners of his eyes crinkling with warmth. "Guidance was all I could give. Your unity, virtues, and wits did the rest."

Outside, the cathedral bells chimed midnight. Kraus glanced at the door. "My work here is done. But if the Orloj should need you again, I suspect a new call will come."

He gave a mischievous smile, stepping slowly backward. "Until next time, dear Orloj Wizards." His figure blurred gently, then he was gone—faded into the shifting moonbeams, leaving only faint footprints on the ancient flagstones.

Bart turned to Blunt; eyebrows raised. "We… uh… best head back, right? We can catch a late train to London if we hurry."

Blunt nodded. "Yeah… Let's go." He exchanged glances with his mates. They all felt a shared sense: Something bigger awaits—but for now, we rest.

Together, they headed for the cathedral's great doors. Outside, the quiet streets of York unspooled, the night air cool on their faces. In their hearts, a profound serenity glowed—an awareness they had touched a deeper magic, forging them into Orloj Wizards.

On the Way to King's Road

As they boarded the near-empty train back to London, the Harlequins sank into their seats with relieved grins. Bart and Antonella settled a few rows behind, dozing off after a long night. Midway through the journey, Reddish nudged Checkered, pointing out the window. Outside, beneath flickering station lights, a swirl of color coalesced—Mrs. V., clad in fluttering scarves, was waving gently at them, invisible to all but the six. Breezie suppressed a joyous laugh. No one else in the carriage reacted. Within seconds, she dissolved into the dawn mist, leaving the Harlequins snickering at the wonder of it all: illusions that only they—Orloj Wizards—could see.

Dawn Over London

In a final swirl of mundane travel, the train pulled into **King's Cross Station** at the edge of daybreak. The six Harlequins blinked as alongside Bart and Antonella, they emerged onto the platform, exhausted yet triumphant. Crisp birdsong cut through the hush—**the city stirring to a new day**, unaware of the illusions that had twisted through the night.

A chorus of familiar voices rose in relief. **All their parents and guardians, rushed forward**, eyes brimming with emotion at the sudden reappearance of their children. For the other five families, it was the first glimpse of the Harlequins since that tense goodbye at the train station. They had barely sensed any lapse in time—**to them, it felt like moments**—but the worry etched on their faces revealed how every second had weighed heavily.

"Goodness, you look—different," one of the mothers whispered, **eyes shining with tears** as she pulled Breezie into a tight embrace.

"Are you hurt? What happened?" a father asked Firee, placing both hands on his son's shoulders, searching his gaze.

As the group reunited, **Checkered's mother tried to hide a trembling laugh**, hugging her daughter, while **Reddish's father** clapped her on the back, scanning for injuries. **Greenie's parents** wiped tears, overjoyed to see her radiant with new confidence. **Firee** squeezed his father's hand in a quiet show of reassurance. Through it all, the Harlequins felt a profound swirl of gratitude; these were the people who trusted them despite the mysteries.

Breezie, Greenie, Reddish, Firee, and Checkered then exchanged glowing smiles with Blunt. The **bond of Orloj**

Wizardry sparkled in each gaze, an unspoken testament to the illusions they had bested and the unity that had triumphed.

"We're... okay," Checkered finally murmured, hugging her mother again. "Better than okay, actually."

Seeing **all** the parents drawn together, Bart and Antonella let out matching sighs of relief, tension draining from them at last. They might never fully grasp the night's events, but in that dawn-light courtyard, **love and relief** overshadowed every unanswered question.

Across the station's windows, a faint reflection showed a **raven** perched on a distant lamp post, its uncanny gaze meeting theirs. For an instant, it reflected the Orloj's face in its glossy eye, then cawed and flew off, leaving them to greet the fresh promise of a London sunrise.

They were **Orloj Wizards** at last.

Days later, as the Harlequins dispersed to their homes, Blunt felt the Orloj's hum linger in his chest, drawing him across the sea to Boston's ancient embrace.

Boston, Massachusetts (Fall 2034)

A crisp wind blew through the old city streets, rustling golden leaves across the cobblestones. In a secluded courtyard outside a historic library, two hooded figures conversed in hushed tones, their postures betraying impatience.

"The rumor is they might come here next," one figure said, voice muffled by the hood. "The Harlequins. Word spreads quickly among certain circles. The Orloj's chosen ones are unstoppable… unless, of course, we intercept them first."

A low chuckle followed, echoing ominously in the courtyard's dusk. "Boston's old magic runs deep. They won't slip past us if they attempt another quest here."

Meanwhile, halfway across the city, inside a bustling café near Beacon Hill, Blunt Cromwell-Smith closed his phone after a brief call with Reddish. He glanced at a battered old map of Massachusetts pinned on the wall. Something about the lines of the coastline and the ancient folk tales scrawled in the margins drew his eye.

He sensed the Orloj's presence stirring again—faint but insistent.

Another puzzle? Another threat?

He exhaled softly, remembering how each city's hidden clock revealed deeper illusions.

Courage, generosity, humility…all the virtues might be tested once more.

Pocketing a small, archaic key—one he'd found inside Kraus's final gift—Blunt smiled to himself. His aunt and uncle had teased him about "settling down" for a normal year in Boston. Yet old libraries and cryptic references to newly uncovered magical doors hinted that *normal* would not last.

Outside, the sun dipped behind the centuries-old steeples, painting the sky with pink and gold. Blunt stepped into the street, **Orloj Wizard** insignia thrumming under his jacket. Somewhere in Boston's labyrinth of colonial streets and hidden tunnels, new illusions likely lurked. He would be ready—*they* all would be.

With a determined grin, he set off into the gathering twilight, already feeling that subtle hum of the Orloj in the crisp autumn air. For the Harlequins, another chapter was about to begin.

Central Institute of Arts and Literature (Fall 2058)

The last lines of Erasmus's narrative fade into the hush of the auditorium. Five hundred students, plus the VR attendees, sit spellbound, processing the extraordinary vision of illusions and virtues he has just shared from decades-past London.

Onstage, **Professor Erasmus Cromwell-Smith II** exhales slowly, setting aside his notes. His deep burgundy tweed suit seems to glow in the spotlight. For a moment, he stands in thoughtful silence, letting the tension dissolve—just as, years ago, he and his friends stood victorious at the Tower of London.

A ripple of soft applause spreads. Then, from the back row, a lone voice exclaims, *"Insanely awesome!"*—triggering a delighted laugh from the entire hall. Professor Cromwell-Smith smiles, remembering how that phrase echoed at the close of every Orloj quest.

"Thank you," he says gently, projecting warm gratitude across the auditorium. "You've walked with me through illusions, betrayals, and triumphs. In London, my companions and I passed beyond Master Wizards, taking on responsibilities we had never imagined. We left the city changed forever."

He adjusts his glasses, a nostalgic glimmer in his eye. "But that wasn't the end. Not of our wizarding legacy, nor of the Orloj's watchful presence."

A soft murmur stirs among the students—some anticipating a next book, others simply awed.

"You see," Erasmus continues, voice dipped in mystery, "the Orloj has many faces. And in time, it called us to a new realm…which, ironically, was much closer to my hometown than any of us could have guessed."

He lets the words hang, checking his watch in mock exasperation. The time reads seven minutes past the hour—tradition. A gentle hush settles, as though the entire hall stands on the cusp of another revelation.

"That," he says, eyes dancing with secret delight, "is a tale for next semester. Until then—thank you for joining me on this London chapter. May your hearts remain open to illusions and virtues alike…for they often appear in the most unexpected places."

He steps away from the podium to thunderous applause, students rising in excitement. The overhead lights brighten, the

VR screens flicker with a flood of "thank you" messages. Within moments, the swirl of end-of-class chaos begins—yet a lingering sense of wonder remains.

At the side exit, **Lynn Tabernaki** appears, her expression half playful, half curious. She falls in step beside him as he shoulders his satchel.

"So," she teases, "you left them hanging again."

He chuckles. "I did. Not everything is told in one breath, my love. Some mysteries are worth savoring."

They share a smile. With final waves to the departing students, the two slip out the doors and into the crisp California evening.

Epilogue:

Scottish Cottage
(Later that Autumn)

Mist settles over the rugged cliffs of the Isle of Skye, nearly mirroring the hush that descends in the cozy cottage lounge. **Professor Erasmus Cromwell-Smith II** and **Lynn** have returned there for a brief respite, the fireplace crackling softly in the dim light.

Outside, the wind whistles across heather-covered hills, echoing the lonely seabirds' cries. Inside, Lynn sips tea, observing Erasmus's thoughtful silence with practiced affection. On the table, a worn map of **Boston** is spread open, edges curled from use.

"So…" Lynn ventures, eyeing the annotated margin. "Boston, next?"

Erasmus nods slowly, running a fingertip across an old, circled address in the city's heart. "I feel it stirring—an echo of the Orloj's magic. Something older than the cobblestones. Something that might be calling us back."

Lynn sets down her teacup, excitement sparking in her gaze. "And you think your old Harlequin friends will answer that call as well?"

"We still keep in touch," Erasmus says with quiet certainty. "They've sensed tremors—signs that illusions are awakening on my native soil."

He lingers on a memory from the Tower of London—**Bart** and **Antonella** hugging him upon his return, half convinced only minutes had passed. He recalls that luminous moment of becoming an Orloj Wizard. The sense that, one day, the Orloj might require them again.

"It's time," he murmurs, clearing his throat. "Time to see if the city that raised me—where my father taught me everything—will soon become the next stage for illusions and virtues. I suspect the Orloj is never truly finished with us."

Rising from his chair, Erasmus crosses to the window, where a silvery moon illuminates the restless Atlantic. The reflection in the glass fleetingly resembles that swirl of clock gears he once saw in London's Big Ben.

"We're not done yet," Lynn remarks gently, sidling up to him, hand in his. "Another dive into your wizarding past, yes?"

He smiles, heart brimming with anticipation and a faint tingle of caution. "I'd say so. Let's see where the Orloj leads."

Erasmus wrote, *"Illusions cloak every era—greed in gold, pride in screens—yet virtues pierce them still, as they did for us, a light for all who seek."*

Outside, a gust of wind rattles the old cottage door, as though knocking for permission. Beyond the cliffs, the ocean's endless horizon promises new journeys—both real and magical. Erasmus sighed, his quill tracing truths: virtues bloom where illusions fade, a legacy etched in time's tender embrace.

PARTING WORDS BY THE AUTHOR

We have crossed the final threshold in a place thought to lack any great astrological clock—and discovered more illusions than all prior quests combined. London's hidden Orloj tested every virtue the Harlequins gathered: humility, loyalty, respect, generosity, perseverance, and more. Here, illusions became intimate reflections of their inner doubts, forcing each triumph to be anchored in unity. Now the grand cycle closes—yet the clock's spirit never truly ends. Time churns on; illusions arise again; the Goblin's shadow, or our own flaws, might still lurk. But you, dear reader, have glimpsed how these wizards overcame each moral trial. Take heart. Whenever the next challenge appears, remember that the Orloj's final gift is this: with clear virtues at our side, we can outlast even the most relentless illusions.

—Erasmus Cromwell-Smith II.

Table of Contents (Detailed)

Author's Note
A warm welcome from Erasmus Cromwell-Smith II, hinting that London—though lacking a famous astronomical clock—conceals great mysteries.

Preface: Isle of Skye, Scotland (Summer 2058)
Erasmus and Lynn reflect on past wizarding trials. London looms in Erasmus's memory as a uniquely challenging city.

Central Institute of Arts and Literature (Fall 2058)
Erasmus begins his annual course, finally revealing the full story of London's hidden Orloj.

Prologue (Summer 2033)
- The Harlequins (Blunt, Reddish, Firee, Checkered, Breezie, Greenie) sense a magical pull toward London.
- Subtle illusions appear across the city; ghostly mentors hint at a new Orloj.
- The Dark Goblin lurks, eager to exploit lingering flaws.

Chapter 1: Arrival & Ominous Encounters
- Reunion at King's Cross.
- Illusions immediately test them; the Dark Goblin taunts their uncertainty.
- Parents and chaperones watch from the edges, unaware of deeper magic.

Chapter 2: The Quest for London's Astrological Clock
- Following cryptic clues, the group travels to Hampton Court Palace and several English cathedrals (Wells, Exeter, Norwich, Leicester, York Minster).
- Realization that Big Ben itself houses London's hidden Orloj, though "invisible" to ordinary eyes.

Chapter 3: Under the Shadow of Big Ben
- The Harlequins cross into Parallel London, an enchanted overlay.
- The Orloj speaks: they have **24 hours** to surpass their Master Wizard level, or illusions will consume them.
- The Dark Goblin steps up his pursuit.

Chapter 4: First Tower Illusion
Virtue: Generosity vs. **Flaw:** Indifference
- **Mentor: Cornelius Tetragor**
- Through poems/stories ("Flowers From The Heart," "The Magical City Busker"), they learn that caring deeds overcome apathy.
- Gain an item (often a "lens" or "charm") revealing heartlessness in illusions.

Chapter 5: Lost in the Labyrinth
Virtue: Kindness vs. **Flaw:** Callousness / Grudges
- **Mentor: Lazarus Zeetrikus**
- Poems/fables ("Kindness," "The Street Vendor From Portoviejo") underscore compassion—especially toward those who've wronged you.
- They refine a protective empathy that repels cruelty-based illusions.

Chapter 6: Breakfast with the Orloj
- No "new" virtue taught; the Orloj insists on using existing powers swiftly.
- Mrs. V. whisks them into classic British children's tales (Peter Pan, Mary Poppins, etc.), illustrating how childlike wonder combats illusions.

Chapter 7: Shadows of Sloth
Virtue: Perseverance vs. **Flaw:** Sloth / Giving Up
- **Mentor: Lettizia Dillettante**

- A trio of poem-like meditations on Discipline, Impetus, and Perseverance show how unwavering resolve is built from smaller habits.
- The Harlequins learn to conquer mental fatigue illusions.

Chapter 8: Shadows of Arrogance
Virtue: Humility vs. **Flaw:** Pride / Ego
- **Mentor: Lucrecia Van Egmond**
- **Featured Short Story:** "The Fall of Lord Avenhurst". A cautionary tale about tyranny undone by pride.
- The Harlequins receive the "Mirror of Humility," which breaks illusions of self-importance.

Chapter 9: Twilight's Summons — The Orloj's Second Counsel
- The Orloj warns them again: illusions are fastest to exploit hesitation or pride.
- A cameo trip to Shakespeare's Globe underscores creativity outliving illusions.

Chapter 10: Echoes of Loyalty
Virtue: Loyalty vs. **Flaw:** Betrayal / Broken Trust
- **Mentor: Paulina Tetrikus**
- Poems like "The Crown of Loyalty" and "The Magic in The Light of A New Day" (no **Avenhurst** references here) remind them that hearts united repel illusions of disloyalty.

Chapter 11: Shadows of Betrayal
Virtue: Tenacity vs. **Flaw:** Resignation / Hopelessness
- **Mentor: Morpheus Rubicom**
- Writings "Tenacity" and "What Is Greatness" highlight unbreakable drive to keep going, no matter how illusions say "quit."

Chapter 12: The Final Chime

- The Goblin attacks with illusions in Parallel London's streets, trying a last time to wear them down.
- They unite all virtues to hold him at bay; the Orloj calls them to the Tower for one culminating challenge.

Chapter 13: The Tower of London Challenge

- **Six final trials,** each overseen by an illusory mentor matching the virtue they originally taught:
    1. **Generosity (Cornelius)**
    2. **Kindness (Lazarus)**
    3. **Perseverance (Dillettante)**
    4. **Humility (Van Egmond)**
    5. **Loyalty (Paulina)**
    6. **Tenacity (Morpheus)**
- By passing all six, they ascend to **Orloj Wizards**, a new rank beyond Master Wizard.

Epilogue

- They emerge at dawn, families relieved.
- Frame stories (Scottish cottage, 2058) show Erasmus reflecting on how London changed them and hinting that Boston might be next.

Author's Parting Words

Poems & Fables Index

Note: Chapters 6 and 9 also feature cameo "fables" drawn from children's classics or Shakespeare but do not contain full poems/fables in the same sense.

About the Author,

Erasmus Cromwell-Smith is an American Writer, Playwright, Poet, and Pedagogue. He's published 32 books in the genres of self-help, poetry, young-adults, education, and sci-fi.